Miles from you

JORDAN SHORE

Copyright © 2020 **Jordan Shore**

This book or any portion thereof may not be reproduced or used in any manner whatsoever without the express permission of the publisher except in the use of brief quotations in a book review.

All rights reserved

First edition published 2020

CONTENTS

Chapter 1 1
Chapter 2 5
Chapter 3 7
Chapter 4 11
Chapter 5 19
Chapter 6 25
Chapter 7 29
Chapter 8 31
Chapter 9 33
Chapter 10 41
Chapter 11 43
Chapter 12 49
Chapter 13 51
Chapter 14 55
Chapter 15 59
Chapter 16 61
Chapter 17 65
Chapter 18 75
Chapter 19 79
Chapter 20 83
Chapter 21 87

Chapter 22 93
Chapter 23 103
Chapter 24 107
Chapter 25 109
Chapter 26 111
Chapter 27 115
Chapter 28 119
Chapter 29 123
Chapter 30 131
Chapter 31 137
Chapter 32 141
Chapter 33 145
Chapter 34 153
Chapter 35 155
Chapter 36 161
Chapter 37 165
Chapter 38 169
Chapter 39 171
Chapter 40 175
Chapter 41 179
Chapter 42 185
Chapter 43 187

CHAPTER 1

LEXI

"Babe, grab the popcorn. The movie's about to start!" my boyfriend, Tyler, yells from the living room.

I laugh, grab the bag off the counter, and walk into the room. I sit on the couch next to him as he wraps his arm around me. He takes a handful of buttered popcorn and shoves it into his mouth.

"So, what movie are we watching?" I ask.

"Only the best movie of all time, It Chapter 2," he tells me.

I look at him. "Really Ty? You know I don't like scary movies."

"Don't worry babe, I'll protect you," he teases me.

I chuckle and turn my attention to the movie. I love Tyler, I really do. We met two years ago as sophomores. He and his friends were shoving each other in the hallway when someone pushed Tyler into me, knocking all of my books out of my hands, along with my glasses. He stayed to help me pick them up and found out I was in the same class as him. He got my number, one thing led to another, and here we are.

I guess you could say Tyler and I defied all odds for high school. He was the star quarterback and I was just some girl on the debate team. And the math team. Oh, and the science league. When Tyler first asked me on a date, I said no. I was too scared. Why was he asking me when he could get any girl in this school? However, Tyler kept asking me and asking me, and finally I gave in. The first day we held hands at school, everyone was staring at us. I heard whispers behind my back, people laughed at me, and everyone thought it was a joke. He purposely would kiss me in front of people to show that we were serious. I don't care anymore, though. I'm with Tyler, and I wouldn't want to be with anyone else.

My phone rings, and without even looking I know exactly who it is.

"Let me guess, your mom," Tyler says.

I look at my phone and, sure enough, it's my mom. I hit the decline button and slide my phone in my back pocket. She probably wants me home. Every time I'm with Tyler she always calls to make sure I'm not doing something stupid, like getting pregnant. For some reason she doesn't trust Tyler.

As the movie finishes I look at the time. Wow, it's after eleven, I think to myself. I take the popcorn bag and throw it away.

"You pig! You finished the whole bag," I tease him.

"Hey, I wasn't the only one eating it," he says before kissing my forehead.

"Well, I gotta go. My mom is probably freaking out right now," I tell him. He pulls me into his arms and hugs me tight.

"Do you have to go? It's a Friday night," he tells me.

"I know babe, but have you met my mother?" I ask him.

Of course he had met my mom, and he should know that she is extremely strict. I love my mom, but she drives me insane. She has a whole life plan for me, which involves me attending Harvard and becoming a lawyer. She has strong opinions about Tyler, and she isn't afraid to share them. She thinks he's a bad influence on me, but I obviously disagree. What she doesn't know is that Tyler and I have a plan of our own. He already has a full ride to Sacramento State in California, which I'm very proud of, while I plan on attending USC in the fall. The schools are only ten minutes apart, which means we don't have to leave each other. I'm very excited for the future with Tyler.

"You can sleep over. My mom won't mind," he says with a smile.

"Yeah, well I think my mom would mind. I love you. See you soon, alright?" I say.

"You betcha. Love you, too."

I give him a quick kiss then run out of the door before he can say anything else.

CHAPTER 2

TYLER

I watch Lexi run out of my house and into her car. She is so terrified of her mom, but if she was my mom, I would be terrified, too. I head back upstairs only to be call into my mom's room.

"Did Lexi leave?" my mom asks me.

"Yeah, she did," I tell her.

"How did she take it?"

"Um, I haven't exactly told her yet," I say. She sighs and takes off her reading glasses.

"Tyler, you promised you were going to tell her tonight. We are leaving in ten days, and it isn't fair to her that she doesn't know."

"I know, I just haven't found the right time."

"Well, you better find the right time. Now get some sleep. Love you," she says.

"Love you too, goodnight, mom."

I walk into my room and take my shirt off. I crawl into bed, but

I can't sleep. Lexi is going to kill me when she finds out. How do you tell someone you love that you're moving? I found out over the summer that my mom got this great job opportunity in Westport, Connecticut. We found a house just a couple blocks away from where she will be working.

I'm bummed to be moving out of this amazing town. There is so much to do here, and I really do wish we didn't have to leave. There's a beautiful park five minutes from our house that Lexi and I go to all the time, with a gorgeous lake right in the middle surrounded by trees and bushes. Lexi and I love taking our pictures there. Well, it's more just me taking pictures of her. Oh, and who can forget all the shops and restaurants that are in the center of town? There are a couple of little boutiques lined up all along the roads. My mom went to the boutiques all the time to get useless junk we never touched. But, my mom needs this job. My dad left out of the blue and hasn't been in our lives in over ten years, and it's been really rough for her. One morning he packed up his things and just walked out of the door. I was seven. I remember sitting on the couch and watching my mom burst into tears as he left, begging him not to go. So, I'm actually the one that encouraged her to take the new job.

We already contacted the football coach from my new high school, and he said that I was allowed to come and try out with the team. We drove to Connecticut back in July to see if I was good enough to play varsity, and I am. I'm relieved I'm still able to play football my senior year, but there's only one problem: Lexi. We are supposed to start our senior year next week, and I have no idea how I'm going to tell her that I won't be here. I really don't want us to break up.

We will be able to make this long distance relationship work, right?

CHAPTER 3

LEXI

I open the door to my house and find my mom sitting in the living room.

"Alexa, what do you think you're doing out so late? You're an hour past your curfew," she says in a stern voice.

"I'm sorry, but Tyler and I—"

"Do not mention that boy in this house. He is not good enough for you. Never has been, never will be," she says crossing her arms.

"You don't know that. Tyler is a good person. I love him and he loves me," I fight back.

"Look who you've become. Why can't you be more like your sister? Ugh, I can't even look at you anymore. Go to bed," she says to me.

I want to fight back. I want to tell her that she's an awful mother and I can't wait to get out of here and go to college, but I don't. Instead, I bite my tongue and do as I am told. As I get into bed I think about my sister, Amelia. She's currently a sophomore at Yale, and my mom absolutely adores her. My dad went to Yale and my mom went to Harvard, and they both want us to follow in their footsteps. Amelia already did her part, so now it's my turn. No pressure at all.

I wake up to my alarm going off at 6:30 in the morning. I'm not allowed to sleep in since my mom thinks it's a waste of time. She says I could be studying instead of sleeping. For such a smart woman, I don't understand how she doesn't realize that rest is very important for a teenager. Anyways, I go downstairs and grab an apple. My mom's car isn't in the driveway, so I assume she probably went to the gym. I head back upstairs and take out my book I've been reading, A People's History of the United States. At around nine, my phone rings. I smile when I see it's Tyler.

"Hey babe," I say through the phone.

"Hey beautiful, you busy?"

"Not really. I'm just studying. What's up?" I ask.

"Can I steal you for the day, or will your mom not let you leave the house?"

"My mom's not here," I tell him.

"Great. I'll pick you up in 20 minutes."

He hangs up the phone, and I quickly get changed into jeans and a sweater.

About 20 minutes later, I hear a honk. Even though I knew it was coming, it still makes me jump. I run outside and hop in the front seat of his car.

"Hey," he says, leaning over to kiss me.

"So, what's the plan for today?" I ask him. He pulls out of my driveway.

"Maybe we can go to the mall? I know you wanted some new clothes. Then later tonight, my guy Jace is throwing a party. We can swing by and hang out," Tyler suggests. I look at him out of the corner of my eye.

"A party? Tyler, that's your thing. I don't want to be standing there all by myself while you're getting wasted," I pout.

"Babe, you know I can't leave your side for more than two minutes. I promise I won't drink. Besides, I haven't had a drink in months," he says, smiling. His knuckles brush over my leg, making me blush. Tyler knows how to make me feel safe and comfortable. There is nothing he could do that would make me ever want to leave him.

"I love you so much," I say and lean over to kiss his cheek.

CHAPTER 4

TYLER

I pull into a parking spot at the mall and open the car door for Lexi. She thanks me and grabs my hand as we walk inside. I hate coming to the mall. I'm basically the only guy in here, and the rest are teenage girls who buy slutty clothes. Except my girlfriend. Lexi only wears sweaters and jeans, and it's what I love about her. She doesn't care or worry about what other people think, and she doesn't like showing off her body to get attention. Every girl I have hooked up with before Lexi is the complete opposite.

She drags me into Forever 21 and starts looking at some jeans. As I'm sitting there watching this beautiful girl gush over the clothes, an idea hits me. This is my chance. I have to tell her that I'm leaving. It's a public place, so she can't throw that big of a tantrum. I take a deep breath. Alright, here goes nothing.

"So listen, there's something I need to tell you," I say.

"What's up?" she asks me.

"Well, um, see the thing is—" I get interrupted by her phone ringing. She takes it out of her back pocket.

"Hold on one sec, it's my stupid mother." She rolls her eyes and answers it.

"Hi mom," she says. After a couple of "okays" and a "goodbye," she finally hangs up.

"So, my mom is going to Yale to visit my sister, so she won't be home till tomorrow," Lexi tells me.

"Oh great," I say.

"Oh my god, look at these jeans. I'm gonna try them on." She grabs them from off the rack and races towards the dressing room. Well, there goes my chance of telling her.

After we're done shopping, we go to Wendy's for lunch. I personally hate this place, but Lexi's stomach was growling, and she loves it. She takes a bite out of her cheeseburger and swallows it.

"Babe, I really need to talk to you," I say.

"Is everything okay? You seemed a little on edge at the mall," she asks, taking a bite out of her cheeseburger.

"Yeah, everything's fine. It's just kind of important," I say.

"Tyler?" a male voice says, walking up from behind me. I turn around. You have got to be kidding me.

"Dude, what's up man!" Brady says, giving me a bro hug.

"Nothing much. You coming to the party tonight?" I ask.

"Are you kidding? Of course I am. You know I never miss a party." He turns to face my girlfriend. "Sup, Lexi."

"Hey."

"I've got to go, but I'll see you tonight," he says to me.

"Right, see ya," I say, before sitting back in my seat. I look at Lexi, and I can tell something's wrong.

"Are you okay?" I ask her.

"Tyler, I'm not feeling so well," Lexi says while clutching her stomach.

"Okay, come here," I help her up and she holds on to me while trying her best not to throw up all over the tiled floor.

We decide to go back to Lexi's house. Usually I would never come to her house, mainly because her mom terrifies me, but since she isn't here... I was more than happy to come. She takes some medicine to calm her upset stomach and about 30 minutes later, she's back to her happy self.

"I can't believe you still have this picture," I laugh while looking at the picture next to her bed. It was a picture of us as sophomores, on our first date to the zoo. She was so nervous. I remember her exact outfit. She wore her hair up in a high ponytail and had a pink skirt on with a black, long sleeve shirt. She looked adorable.

"I think it's cute," she tells me.

"Every picture is cute when you're in it," I say, wrapping my arms around her.

Lexi's beautiful, and the only reason why people don't like her is because she's smart.

People are jealous: They want what she has, but because they don't, they shut her out.

She has gorgeous brown hair and a smile that lights up the room. What's not to love about her?

"Aw babe, you're too sweet," she tells me. I kiss her forehead. All of a sudden she jabs her fingers into the side of my stomach, making me jump back. She giggles and runs to the other side of her bed.

"Oh now you're gonna get it," I say. She sticks her tongue out at me, making me laugh. Man, I love this girl. I jump over her bed and grab her wrists. She attempts to wiggle my hands off, but my hands pin her down.

"You're too strong!" She laughs. I pick her up and gently lay her on the bed, then wrap my knees on either side of her. I manage to hold my weight up, though, so I don't crush her. I start tickling her arms and her stomach, and she bursts into laughter.

"Okay, okay, I give in," she says, still laughing. I stop tickling her.

"Thought so." My lips come crashing on top of hers. Still holding my weight up, I bring my hands to the side of her face.

After about five minutes, I hear the door open and close.

"Alexa, are you home?" I hear her dad yell from the kitchen. I groan, then rest my head on her chest.

"Crap," I hear her whisper.

"I thought your dad wasn't supposed to be home until Monday?" I say to her.

"He wasn't. I'm not supposed to have any boys in my room," she says. "I'll be right down, dad!"

"Do we have to go down?" I ask her. She looks at me.

"Yes, we do. Don't worry, my dad actually likes you. Just act natural," she grabs my hand and drags me downstairs.

"Dad!" Lexi says, hugging him.

"Hi Lexi. I missed you," he says, then looks at me.

"Tyler, I didn't know you were over. What were you two doing?" he asks us. I look at Lexi.

"We were just talking about our summer work for school," Lexi lies.

"Oh, good. I'm glad you take your work just as seriously as Lexi does," her dad says to me.

"Of course I do, sir," I nod my head. I actually don't take school seriously at all, but I'll say whatever it takes to please her dad.

"So, how was your business trip? I thought you weren't going to be home till Monday?" Lexi says.

"Change of plans. They let me off early. Well, I'll be in my room if you need me. I have to unpack and get some rest. I have a lot of work to catch up on tomorrow. Love you, sweetie." And her father disappears.

"Do you think we can stop by my place before the party? I want to change my shirt," I ask her.

"Yeah, of course. I'm just going to grab my purse. I'll be right back." She kisses my cheek then runs upstairs.

"I'm driving," she says, coming back down. She takes her keys off the counter and hurries outside.

"Lexi," I call to her. "My car is here, so I should drive." She shakes her head.

"You can come back with me after the party's over. Let's go," she insists and hops in the driver's seat. Lexi is so stubborn. I sit in the front seat as she pulls out of the driveway and drives to my house.

"So is there going to be a lot of alcohol at this party?" she asks me, her eyes dead focused on the road.

"Probably," I shrug.

"Oh," she says as she shifts around in her seat. That's what Lexi does when she's nervous. She can't sit still.

"C'mon Lexi, it's Jace we're talking about here. Of course there's gonna be alcohol there. But I'll be with you the entire time. Do you trust me?" I ask her.

"You know I do," she answers.

"Then you have nothing to worry about." When she pulls up I tell her to wait and run inside. I quickly take my AC/DC shirt off and throw on a black one. Okay, now I'm ready. I walk back outside and get in the car. She puts her phone down and smiles.

"You good?" she asks me. I nod my head, and she starts driving to Jace's house.

When we pull up to the house, we can already hear the music blasting. I look to Lexi, who looks like she's about to pass out.

"You'll be fine Lexi. I'll be with you the entire time," I reassure her.

"I know babe, I know." She smiles.

I can tell she's trying to hold it together to make me happy, but I feel terrible for dragging her along to this party. I kiss her lips then get out of the car. When I was a sophomore I used to go to parties every weekend. I would get drunk and hookup with random girls. Actually, Lexi is my first real girlfriend. Ever since I met her, It's like I completely changed. I didn't want to go to parties and drink. All I wanted to do was be with her. I honestly thought I would never feel this way about someone. I squeeze her hand as I open the large glass door and we walk in. I'm always surprised by the size of his house. The foyer is as big as my whole home.

We instantly get sucked in by the large crowd of people. There must be hundreds of kids in here. I take Lexi and navigate my way to the kitchen, where we can finally breathe.

"Wow, there are a lot of people here," Lexi says.

I nod my head in agreement. I can tell she's extremely uncomfortable. She has only been to one other party in her entire life, and it actually was before we were dating. I remember watching her the whole night. Lexi doesn't know this, but I've had my eye on her for a long time. Ever since I saw her in her black dress for our 8th grade dance, I knew that she was the one for me.

"Oh my god, Lexi, you came!" I hear Bianca say. She runs up and gives Lexi a hug. Bianca and Lexi became friends last year when they were partnered up for a science project.

"Yeah, it took some convincing, but I'm here," Lexi says, faking a smile.

"Okay, well I'm going to find Skyler, but I'll catch you later," she says before walking away.

"Wanna dance?" I yell over the music. She nods her head and we walk to the living room. I grab Lexi's wrist, twirling her around, and then proceed to kiss her, because we both really don't know how to dance. Out of nowhere someone hits my back, making me jump. Lexi and I both turn our heads.

"Yo man! I can't believe it's your last week here." Jace frowns. My mouth drops.

Oh no. Jace is drunk. I look at Lexi.

"What?" Lexi asks, confused. Jace laughs.

"Dude, you haven't told her? Well, this ought to be good," he says.

"Jace! Shut up," I snap. "It's nothing, Lexi," I say to her.

"It ain't nothing," Jace adds, shaking his head.

"Tyler, what's going on?" she asks me.

"Do you think we can talk about this in private?" I ask, grabbing her arm. She shakes my hand off.

"No, I want to know right now."

"Lexi, please," I beg.

"Get a clue, Lexi. He's moving," Jace slurs. She looks at him, then starts laughing. Well this wasn't the response I thought I was going to get.

"Ha ha, very funny guys. I almost fell for it," Lexi smiles. She looks at me, waiting for me to laugh with her. When I don't say anything, her smile fades.

"He is joking, right?" she asks. I look down to the ground and shake my head.

"Well, when are you leaving?"

"Five whole days!" Jace yells.

"But you're still living in Massachusetts, right?" she asks with a hint of desperation.

"Nope! He's a Connecticut boy now!" Jace answers.

"Shut it, Jace," I say. I finally have enough courage to look at her. It's like my worst nightmare coming true. What have I done?

"Lexi please say something," I say. Instead, she runs through the crowd and out the door.

CHAPTER 5

LEXI

I can feel tears streaming down my face as I search through my bag to find the keys.

"Lexi!" Tyler calls, running after me. I manage to find my keys but Tyler grabs my arms first.

"Get off of me!" I yell at him.

"Please, just listen to me," he says.

"I don't want to listen to anything you have to say. You lied about everything," I sob.

"Lexi, please. I meant to tell you, I really did," he says.

"Yeah, well, you didn't. Instead you lied to me."

"I never meant for it to get this out of hand," he says.

"How could you do this to me? After everything we've been through!" I yell.

"I just didn't want to hurt you," he whispers. I can tell he's trying his best not to cry.

"Well sorry to burst your bubble, but that's exactly what you did." I shake his arm off mine and climb in the car, not looking back for even a second.

When I get home, I run inside and slam my bedroom door. I put my face into my pillow and scream. Thank god my dad is a heavy sleeper. I don't feel like explaining what happened. Tyler didn't have the courage to tell me, and I found out from Jace. Jace! What if he wasn't drunk? Would Tyler have even told me? I could seriously punch him right now. I can't believe my mom was right. I change into my pajamas and wrap a blanket around myself. I feel sick to my stomach. All this time he's been lying to me, and I was too dumb to notice. I hate myself. Shouldn't I be hating him? I honestly don't even know. All I know is that I don't ever want to see his smug face ever again.

The next morning I wake up to five missed calls and ten text messages from him. I delete them all without even reading one. I look outside the window. His car is gone. I walk downstairs and my dad is standing in the kitchen wearing a suit.

"Hi, Alexa. How was last night?" he asks me.

"It was fine," I lie. "I'm gonna spend the rest of the day in my room making sure I have everything ready for school," I inform him.

"Okay, well have fun. I have to run into the office for a couple of hours but your mother should be home in a bit," my dad says. I nod my head and walk upstairs to my room and take out my notebooks from my desk.

About two hours later, I hear the door open and close. *Great, mom's home.* I hear footsteps upstairs and a light knock on my door.

"Alexa, can I come in?" she asks me.

"Yes," I reply. She opens the door and sits next to me on my bed.

"Amelia says hi," she tells me.

"Great," I say grumpily as I roll my eyes.

"Is everything okay?"

I close my textbook. "Oh, don't act like a caring mother now," I say. Oh my god, did I just say that to my own mom? What is wrong with me?

"Alexa I might not agree with everything you're doing, but I am still your mother," she says in a steady voice.

"I'm not really in the mood to talk. So if you don't mind, I'm going to get back to taking out the post-its from this book," I say, reopening my textbook.

"Alright, well I'll be downstairs making chicken and broccoli," she says to me. She stands up and looks at me. "Dinner will be ready in two hours. I expect the table to be made." She rubs the wrinkles out of her perfectly white blouse and walks out of my room.

* * *

It's been a couple of days since I've seen or talked to Tyler. He's tried to call and text me numerous times, but I haven't replied back. Today is the first day of Waltham High, and I'm already dreading it. I really don't want to go to school. Do I even have to go? Tyler is leaving for Connecticut tomorrow, and I am still so beyond hurt that he's been lying to me. I walk downstairs and make myself a bowl of cereal. My mom comes walking down in a purple pencil skirt and a dark green blouse. Her hair is in a tight bun, as always.

"I have to go. I have a lot of meetings at work today, so I will not be available if you need me. Please don't be late for school," she says and then leaves the house.

I put the bowl in the sink, then go back to my room and get changed into jeans and a camouflage tee shirt. I head to the bathroom to finish getting ready. This is the first time in a while that I'm going to school without someone by my side. I wonder if everyone knows what happened. I'm sure they do. I mean, I did find out that he was leaving at a party. I pull into the parking lot and get out of the car, grabbing my backpack. I face the school and notice a boy who looks an awful lot like Tyler standing at the bottom of the stairs. Oh my god. It is Tyler. When he notices me, he stands up straight and rubs his hand through his hair. I look around, trying to find an escape route, but there is none. My only option is to walk past Tyler. I start speed walking through the parking lot and try to pass him, but he manages to grab my arm and pull me to him.

"What?" I snap.

"I need to talk to you," Tyler says.

"Yeah, well, I don't need to talk to you."

"Lexi, stop, please. I know I screwed up. What I did was so wrong and I get that, but don't shut me out."

"Don't you get it, Tyler? I trusted you with my whole heart and all you did was break it." I try my best not to cry as a group of freshmen walks past us.

"You know I would never hurt you. I need you, Lexi. Please just give me another chance," he begs.

"See, Tyler, that's the thing. I can't forgive you. I don't trust you anymore, and I don't think I ever will." He drops my arm and I start to back away.

"So, what now, huh? Are you breaking up with me?" I turn back to face him, tears now filling my eyes. I gulp.

"Yeah, I guess I am. Have fun in Connecticut," I struggle to say. I adjust the backpack on my back, then turn and walk away.

* * *

It's been two weeks since I broke up with Tyler, but it feels like two years. I haven't seen or talked to him since he left. I didn't know how lonely it was going to be without him. I force myself out of bed, throw on gray sweats and my favorite Red Sox sweatshirt, and drive myself to school. As I climb up the steps to what feels like hell, I see Bianca standing by the door. She walks over to me and gives me a hug.

"I haven't seen you in so long. How are you?" she asks, giving me a warm smile.

"Fine," I lie.

"C'mon, I've been through more breakups than you can count. I know for a fact that you're not fine," she tells me.

"Okay, I'm not fine. I'm a complete mess." I start to cry.

"Do you know what always helps me when I'm going through a breakup?"

"What?"

"A party! And you're just in luck. Jace is hosting another one this weekend. He's a real party animal," she gushes.

"Yeah, no, Bianca, I don't really think that's a good idea. The last thing I need right now is to go to a party."

"It'll be fun. You can get drunk and dance…it'll totally take your mind off of Tyler," she says.

"But I don't drink," I point out.

"Well, maybe it's time you should," she says.

I smile and puff out my chest. "You know what? Yeah, I'll go. Pick me up at eight."

Maybe this is a sign. Maybe breaking up with Tyler is a good thing. He was my first date, my first kiss, my first everything. Just because Tyler isn't here anymore doesn't mean I can't have a good time. Maybe it is time to move on.

"Hey, Bianca," Logan says, walking up to her.

"Hey," Bianca responds, blushing. I roll my eyes and laugh inside. The whole school knows that Logan and Bianca have been crushing on each other since forever. They just won't admit it.

"Well, I think that's my cue to leave," I say.

"I'll see you later, alright? I promise you're going to have fun Saturday," Bianca says.

"Okay, well I'm trusting you. I'll see you around, Logan." I walk past the both of them into school.

CHAPTER 6

TYLER

I am not okay. How can Lexi break up with me after everything we've been through? I have not been the same without her. I need her. She kept me sane. Without her, I feel lost. I wonder if she feels the same way? I wonder if she is devastated and is missing me as much as I miss her? I bet she is thinking about me right now. After all, I was the only person she ever hung out with. I bet she wishes she never broke up with me. Maybe I should give her a call right now just to see how she's doing. She can't hate me forever. She probably already got over it. I whip my phone out of my pocket and click on her name. It rings once, then twice, then three times. *C'mon Lexi pick up.*

Finally, it stops ringing.

"Tyler?" Lexi says in her sweet, innocent voice.

"Hey, yeah, it's me. What are you up to?" I ask her.

"Walking home from school. My car is in the shop," she tells me.

My heart breaks a little. I always gave her rides home from school.

"Oh, okay," is all that comes out of my mouth. *Really Tyler? That's the best you could think of? 'Oh, okay?'*

"Is there a reason that you called, Tyler?" she says in a much more serious tone.

"I just wanted to hear your voice," I tell her.

"Okay, well I have to go now. Oh, and please don't call again." She hangs up, and I just stare at my phone. We used to talk for hours . How can she do this to me? We were so good together, and now she's acting like she hates me. I throw my phone off to the side and put my palm against my forehead. What am I going to do? My idiotic friends come marching in my room, making me jump.

"Hey, Tyler, where were you today?" Danny asks.

"Yeah, I thought you were coming to the gym with us," Andrew says.

"Sorry guys, my mind's just not into that kind of stuff right now," I tell them.

"You still into that Lexi chick?" Ben asks. I nod my head.

"Dude, get over her. There are some hot cheerleaders here. They are ten times hotter than Lexi. Even though Lexi is pretty hot," Andrew says.

"Yeah, I wouldn't mind tapping some of that," Danny laughs. I roll my eyes.

"How did you guys even get in my house?" I ask.

"Your mom let us in. Seriously though, Tyler, forget about her. You're in Connecticut now. Can't you just have a little fun?" Ben asks.

"Well, what if I don't want to forget about her?"

Andrew shrugs. "You're going to have to eventually. C'mon guys, let's leave Mr. Grumpy here by himself. Burgers are on me," he says.

"Catch ya later, Tyler," Ben says before the three of them walk out.

I want to punch every single one of them. How dare they make comments about Lexi like that? She's mine, and I know she'll forgive me. I just know she will. I take a deep breath, then put my headphones on. I'm not going to let them get to me.

CHAPTER 7

LEXI

I decide to go to the mall after school. Well, Bianca practically forced me to go. She said I needed to relax and, in her mind, the mall was the best place to do just that. As we're walking around, she stops in front of an arts and crafts store.

"What are you doing?" I ask her.

"Okay, so remember when I dyed my hair purple in the ninth grade?" she asks me. I nod my head. I thought she was crazy when she came walking into school with purple hair. She has beautiful blonde hair and I didn't understand why she would want to change that.

"Well, my older sister did it for me, and she taught me how to do it. Call me crazy, but what if I dyed your hair?" she beams. My eyes go wide.

"Yup, you're crazy."

"C'mon Lexi, live life a little! Stop being so uptight. I promise you'll like it," she begs.

"Bianca, I love my hair. I don't want to change it," I cross my arms.

"Oh my god, it isn't permanent. You can get it out any time you want. I still have the supplies for when I got the purple out of my hair. I bet hot pink would look good," she says touching my hair.

"Bianca..."

"I'm not leaving this spot until you agree," she says, crossing her arms. Wow, Bianca is almost as stubborn as me, and that's saying something.

"Fine, But only at the tips. I'm going to get in so much trouble for this," I tell her.

She smiles.

"Deal," she grabs my arm and runs into the store.

The next day at school I am not feeling confident at all. I feel so different with pink in the tips of my hair and have the feeling everyone keeps looking at me. I'm the good girl in the school, and I bet no one ever thought that I would dye my hair. Heck, I didn't either! I will never forget the horrified expression on my mom's face when she saw me with pink hair. She practically threw a fit! She started yelling at me and told me that I'm throwing away my chances at getting into Harvard. Good thing, because I don't want to go to Harvard. I can't wait to be as far away from my mother as possible. I mean, we live in Waltham, Massachusetts! Harvard is only 20 minutes from where we live. I only mentioned USC to my mom once, and we got in a huge fight about it. The only reason why she let me apply to USC was because she said that I should have a backup school. I'm still planning on going to USC, even though Tyler and I are broken up. I can't live my life for other people anymore.

CHAPTER 8

TYLER

I arrive at the football field, dripping in sweat. From my house to the field, it's five miles. So, instead of driving, I decided to run. When I'm stressed or upset, I like to work out. It keeps my mind off the fact that I no longer have a girlfriend and that it's all my fault. I know I'm a terrible person. I should've talked about it with Lexi as soon as I found out. How could I do this to her? She was the one good thing I had in my life, and I treated her like garbage. She was nothing but sweet and patient with me since the day I met her. I don't deserve her. I walk on the football field where my friends and I are supposed to meet. I wipe the sweat off my forehead and sit on the field.

"Dude, are you even listening to me?" Ben asks. I look at him. I must've spaced out. I didn't even know he was standing right next to me.

"Sorry, what did you say?" I ask him.

"Are you okay? It looks like you just ran a marathon," Ben asks me. He grabs my hand and helps me up.

"Yeah, I'm good. Let's just play," I say.

"Hey guys," Andrew says as he and Danny walk on the field.

"It's about time you guys came," Ben says.

"That chick's staring at you," Andrew says, looking past me. I look in the direction he's looking, and sure enough, there is a blonde-haired girl looking directly at me. "So?"

I shrug

"So, go talk to her," Andrew encourages me. When we lock eyes, she smiles and waves, so I wave back. I feel uncomfortable just looking at another girl. It feels like I'm cheating on Lexi, even though I'm not.

"If you don't go and talk to her, I will," Andrew tells me.

"So go and talk to her. I'm taken," I tell him.

"If by taken you mean dumped, then yeah, I guess you're taken. Suit yourself, I'll talk to her," he says. I roll my eyes and watch him bounce up to her like an idiot. God I wish I didn't come here. I should be at home, finishing up high school with Lexi. I know it was for my mother, and in a way I'm happy that she's finally found herself again, but I can't help but wonder what would've happened if I stayed in Massachusetts with Lexi. There's no point in thinking about that now. What we had was over the minute I started lying to her.

CHAPTER 9

Lexi

I'm getting ready for the party Bianca is forcing me to go to. While we were at the mall, she made me buy an outfit, and as I'm looking at it, I'm not so sure I want to put it on. It's way too revealing. She encouraged me to get a low-cut, tight black shirt that shows my belly button. If Bianca had her way, I would've left the mall with a new belly button piercing. After debating for about ten minutes, I decided to wear it. I'm not trying to impress anyone anymore, and I can do whatever I want.

Bianca honks her horn exactly at eight, and I rush out the door before my mom sees me.

"Lookin' good, Lexi!" Bianca says excitedly.

"Just drive," I order her. She giggles but drives away.

When we arrive at Jace's, it seems more packed than last time. I bite my bottom lip and look at the house, now having second thoughts. I really wish I hadn't come. I don't have my bodyguard with me. He always would protect me. If a guy even looked at me I heard him growl. We get out of the car and Bianca grabs my hand. She hurries on into the house and instantly into the living room where the party is. Bianca finds two red solo cups and hands me one.

"Oh, I don't drink," I wave her off.

"Don't be such a wimp. Try it. It's really good," she encourages me. I reluctantly grab the cup from her hand and smell it. Yuck. It smells disgusting. I look at Bianca as she chugs her drink down. *How did she do that?*

"Drink it," she chants. *You know what, screw it.* I plug my nose and drink the whole cup.

"Woooo!" Bianca yells. She grabs another cup and hands it to me.

"Alright, I'm in. Let's have a good time tonight," I say before putting the cup to my mouth.

After about an hour of dancing and drinking, I'm drunk. Everything seems much more real, if that even makes any sense. I feel like I can do anything. I'm not the shy, scared Lexi anymore. I'm adventures, free, Lexi. I've had one too many cups of alcohol, and now I have to go pee. I stumble over to Jace and tap on his back.

"Jace!" I wave my hand to get his attention. He turns around and smiles.

"Ah, so little miss perfect finally cracked. How's the party life?" he asks me.

"It's fantastic! But I have to go pee. Can you show me where the bathroom is?" I ask him.

"Sure thing. Follow me," he says. I do as I am told and follow him upstairs.

"It's in here," Jace opens the door, allowing me to walk inside. I look around.

Wait... this is a bedroom. I turn around.

"I think you brought me to the wrong room," I tell him.

"No, I don't think so. Have fun!" Jace laughs as he shuts the door, and I hear a lock. Oh my god, I may be drunk, but did Jace just lock me in here? I hear a few other guys join him, and now they're all laughing at me.

"Hey!" I say, hitting the door with all my might. It just makes them laugh even harder.

"What are you guys doing?" I yell. I feel the walls closing in on me. It's like I can't breathe. Tears start streaming down my face. Why am I crying? I knew this was a mistake. I never should have gotten drunk in the first place. I let other people control my life and tell me what to do. I'm smarter than this.

"Let me out, Jace!" I demand. I still hear the guys laughing. Every time I yell, it just makes them laugh even harder. I fall to my knees. I just want to go home. I let my head fall into my lap as I cry. This whole thing is a disaster, and it's all my fault. After Tyler left, it's like I couldn't tell right from wrong. After what felt like an eternity, I hear the doorknob wiggle and the door swings open.

"Lexi?" Bianca gasps. She looks at me, then turns her attention to Jace and his friends.

"What did you guys do?" Bianca asks, crossing her arms.

"Nothing, we were just having a little fun." Jace shrugs.

"You know it was her first time drinking. She was probably scared to death locked in that room," Bianca says.

"Yeah, that was the point," Jace answers. Bianca helps me up.

"You four are losers," Bianca says as we walk past him and his drunk friends. We get outside and Bianca looks at me.

"Are you okay?" she asks me.

"I'm fine. I just want to leave, like right now," I sniff.

"I am so sorry. I never should've made you drink. You were uncomfortable with it from the beginning and I just pushed you to do it. C'mon, I'll drive you home," she says while giving me a hug.

* * *

I am so glad the weekend is over. All Sunday I just sat in my bed and tried to do homework, but even the two cups of coffee didn't help. I never realized I'd feel this crappy after just a few drinks. I was so stupid to think I could fit in at a party. Clearly I'm a terrible drunk, and I don't think I'll be drinking again anytime soon. I'm dreading going back to school. Word had probably spread about what happened to me, and almost everyone would know about me getting locked in a room and having a total meltdown. Itmwill be so embarrassing.

"Lexi, come down here a moment!" I hear my dad yell from downstairs. I groan and throw my computer to the side. I wobble downstairs, trying to hold on to the railing to keep balance. I have never been hung over before, and it's awful. The bright light burns my eyes, and I have a massive headache. I can't focus on anything. I grab onto the seat in front of me and look at both my parents.

"Yes?" I ask them, trying to act normal.

"Lexi, you know how much we care about you, right?" my dad asks. I nod my head.

"We only want what's best for you, which means we're only

going to ask you this once, and we beg of you to not lie. You were out a little late last night, which made us slightly concerned. Where were you last night?" he asks.

"I already told you, I was at Bianca's house studying."

My mom stands up. "Oh, really? See, I told you she would lie," my mom says to my dad.

"What?" I ask, my palms now getting sweaty.

"You missed your curfew, and since you weren't answering your phone, we called Bianca's mother. But when we called, her mother informed us that both you and Bianca were not home. In fact, she told us that Bianca was at a party. So I guess we can only assume that you were with her. And by the looks of you standing in front of us right now, you were definitely with her," my mom says, crossing her arms.

"You were checking up on me? You're kidding, right?" I say.

"Yes, and it's a good thing we did!" my mom answers.

"Oh my god. I'm fricken seventeen! I don't need to be checked up on anymore!

Let me live my life and not be so locked up by you two!" I yell.

"Well, apparently you do still need to be checked up on. How dare you lie to your parents?" my mom looks at my dad, waiting for him to say something.

"Look, your mother's right. You can't lie to us anymore, okay? I hope this was a valuable lesson for you. You may go now," my dad says. I nod my head and walk away.

"David, that's all you have to say?" I hear my mom yell at him. I smile and walk back to my room.

I arrive at school knowing that people would be staring at me, and I was right. I keep my head down the entire time, mortified of what happened this weekend. I was so irresponsible and it never should've happened. I quickly make my way to my locker to grab my books.

"Hey Lexi," Bianca says, coming up next to me.

"Hey," I smile.

"How are you?" she asks sincerely.

"I don't need your pity, Bianca, I'm okay, really," I assure her. As I shove my backpack in my rusty locker, I hear an angry voice down the hall.

"Where is he?" I turn my head, and my heart skips a beat. Tyler? I haven't seen him in almost a month.

"Oh my god," Bianca says. He makes his way towards Jace, and it takes me a second before I realize why he's here. Tyler is going to kill him. He grabs him by the shirt and is about to punch him when I run over there and step in the middle.

"Move, Lexi," Tyler demands.

"No." I cross my arms.

"What did you do to her?" Tyler asks Jace.

"Nothing, man, we just had a little fun with her," he shrugs.

"Really? Because that's not what I heard," he says, his voice getting louder. I grab Tyler's arm.

"Tyler, stop," I tell him. He looks at me, then at Jace, then back at me. After thinking about it, he finally lets go of Jace.

"Thank you," I breathe out. All of a sudden he grabs my arm and pulls me into a janitor's closet. He looks at me up and down.

"You changed your hair," Tyler says while rubbing his neck.

"Yeah, I did." This is so awkward. We used to talk about everything, but now it's like I'm talking to a stranger.

"I want to know what happened," Tyler tells me.

"Nothing happened, alright? It was my fault. I was drunk and—"

"You were drunk? Lexi, are you crazy? What has gotten into you? You change your hair, you go to parties, and now you're getting drunk?!"

"Say it a little louder, I'm not sure the whole school heard you," I say sarcastically.

"Lexi—"

"Why are you here, Tyler? How did you even find out?" I ask him.

"Bianca called me. She told me everything. Why didn't you tell me?" he asks.

"Because you're not my boyfriend anymore. I'm not going to run to you for all of my problems. Tyler, you left me," I answer. He rubs his hand over his face.

"I know, I know. It's just, I like when you come to me with your problems. I miss you. A lot," he says.

"I'm sorry, Tyler, but I've got to get to class. I hope you have a safe drive back," I say coldly. I open the door and walk out, leaving Tyler alone.

CHAPTER 10

TYLER

She hates me. I saw it in her eyes. She basically looked right through me. When Bianca called me and told me what happened, I seriously wanted to kill Jace. How dare he play tricks on her like that? I'm gone for three weeks and he thinks he can do something like that to her? I just have to get Lexi to trust me again. But first things first: I have to make her realize that she still loves me. Deep down, she knows I'm her soulmate.

"Mr. McHale, what are you doing here?" Principal Cooney appears in the doorway, crossing her arms.

"I, uh, I'm just visiting my friends," I lie.

"You are no longer a student here, which means you cannot come on school grounds. You have approximately two minutes to leave before I call the police," she tells me. Jeez, I forgot how tough she is.

"Okay, I'm sorry. I promise I won't cause a scene again." I quickly exit the school and hop in my car. I decide to head over to my old house. I really miss living here. I miss my friends, I miss my house, I miss Lexi – I miss it all. I know I had to move. It was for my mom, who has given up so much for me. It was time I finally gave up something for her, even if it meant losing Lexi. I just wish Lexi would try long distance. I haven't been the same without her. Honestly, I feel like she abandoned me. We promised we would never leave each other, and she left me. Well, technically I left her, but she still broke up with me. I feel hurt more than anything. What point is she trying to make? That I messed up? That I made a mistake? I think we all know that by now.

I pull up to my old house and look at the window where my room used to be. I can see the wall where a picture of me playing football used to hang. I see the corner where my desk used to be. A lot of memories took place in that bedroom. I lost my first tooth, I learned how to read … I had my first kiss with Lexi. I sigh. Why do I always think about Lexi? It's like I can't help it. She was my whole world. I know she still loves me. You can't go from loving someone to hating them. You just can't.

CHAPTER 11

LEXI

I hate him. I truly hate him. How dare he show up at my school and start a fight like that? Then he has the nerve to pull me into the janitors closet! What kind of person does that?

"Alexa, darling, set the table. Your father should be home any minute," my mom says, snapping me out of my thoughts. I nod my head and grab the plates from the cabinet.

"I noticed that you have been distracted lately. I hope that isn't affecting your schoolwork," she tells me while putting the meatloaf and broccoli on the table.

"It's not mom and I'm fine. Can we not talk about my life for once, please?"

"Is it because that boy left, because if it is—"

"Mom, please," I beg. Just then my dad opens the door and puts his briefcase on the counter.

"How was your day?" my mom asks him.

"Very long. Hi, Alexa," my dad says while hugging me.

"Hi dad." I smile and take a seat at the table, and my two parents do the same.

For about half an hour, my dad talks about some big case he's working on while my mom pretends to listen. My mom is the type of person that if it's not about her, she doesn't care. Well, unless it's about Harvard, then she's super invested. But still, that would benefit her if I went to Harvard. So technically, she's only doing this for herself, too.

"So Alexa, I was thinking maybe we can drive up to Harvard this weekend. The last time we were there was about a year ago. We should check it out," my mom says before putting a piece of broccoli in her mouth.

"No thanks, I can just google the campus. I would rather stay here," I tell her.

"Looking up the campus online and actually visiting the place are two different things. We're going, end of discussion. Oh, and wash that pink out of your hair. I don't want you to look trashy when we arrive," she says.

I cross my arms and look at her straight in the eyes. "I'm not going," I say slowly.

She puts her fork down.

"Okay, how about we talk about this later and enjoy this wonderful meal," my dad says, trying to ease the tension between us.

"Alexa Elizabeth Marget, you do not talk like that to me. I am your mother," my mom says, completely ignoring my dad.

"Yeah, and I'm your daughter! You don't even know what I want. Mom, I don't want to go to Harvard," I blurt out. I quickly cover my mouth with my hand but it's too late. I had opened a can of worms.

My mom is pacing back and forth in the living room as I'm watching from the dining table. She looks like she's about to explode into a ball of fire.

"Are you mad?" I ask her.

"Mad? I'm beyond mad! This has been your dream since you were a little girl! I can't believe you're throwing this all away. Is it because of Tyler? That boy will be the death of me."

"It's not about Tyler, mom. It's about me and what I want. I don't want to go to Harvard, and I'm sorry if you don't like it, but it's my choice," I say.

She starts laughing. "Your choice? You think this is your choice? You're just a little girl. I know what's best for you. You're going to Harvard. I did not raise you to be so weak. Gosh, you're not the daughter I thought you were. Clean up the table. I'm taking a shower," she says over her shoulder as she walks away.

Anger starts to build up inside me. My whole life I have been living under the shadow of my mother, but that ends now. Before I know what I'm doing, I throw my shoes on and run out of the house. I have to see him. He is the only one that makes me safe. I know it's wrong, but I need him right now. I knock on the door to his grandparents' house.

"Oh, what a surprise! Hi darling," his grandmother says as she opens the door.

"Hi, Mrs. Adams. Is Tyler here?" I ask.

"Lexi?" Tyler appears from behind his grandmother.

"Can we talk?" I ask him. We sit on the front porch and I tell him everything.

"Lexi, I'm so sorry. You don't deserve to be treated like that," Tyler says as he rubs my back. I try my best not to cry as I feel the cold air hit my face. He wanted to talk inside, but I insisted on sitting on the steps of the porch. I needed the fresh air.

"It's just, she's my mom, you know? I need her in my life. I can't just not have a relationship with her," I tell him.

"I get it. Growing up without a parent sucks," he says. I look out into the open space and sigh.

"Maybe I should just go to Harvard. Would that really be such a bad thing?" I ask as I rest my head on my knuckles.

"No Lexi, you can't go to Harvard. You shouldn't just settle on something just because your mom wants you to go. You deserve to be happy, and if Harvard doesn't make you happy, then don't go. You'll always have me in your corner, even if we're hundreds of miles apart. I mean, I just drove four hours just to beat up a guy that hurt you," he points out.

It makes me feel good knowing that Tyler still doesn't hate me after everything I've said to him. I have tried to hate him, but for some reason I just can't.

"I'm sorry Tyler, I never meant to be so cruel to you. I should never have shut you out like that," I apologize.

Tyler has been so good to me for the past year and a half. He's made me the happiest I've been my entire life, and it wouldn't be fair of me to completely forget everything we've had over a mistake, even if it was as big as lying. Or omitting the truth.

"I really miss you, Lexi. I hope you know that," he says back.

"We aren't getting back together. We can't." I frown.

"Why not? Our love is strong enough to fight this. We can work it out."

"Thank you for talking to me, Tyler, but I really should get going," I stand up and brush the dirt off my pants.

"Lexi," he pleads, standing up and grabbing my hands, but I back away.

"No, Tyler. We can't, okay? Please don't make this any harder than it has to be,"

I say, trying not to get choked up.

"I get it. Let me just give you my new address, for whenever you need a friend to talk to," he says.

"I'm not sure that's a good idea."

"Lexi, put my address in your phone," he demands. After thinking about it, I take my phone out of my pocket and hand it to him. After he finishes, he hands me back my phone.

"I'm sorry, Lexi," he kisses my cheek then walks back inside.

"I'm sorry, too," I whisper once he shuts the door.

CHAPTER 12

TYLER

A week has past, and I'm back to hell. I never wanted to leave Lexi. She was so scared and so sad, but there was nothing I could do to help her. Why? Because we aren't dating anymore. I'm in Connecticut and she's in Massachusetts. God, I miss her so much.

"That girl's staring at you again," Andrew says, throwing me the football. I turn around and, sure enough, it's the same blonde chick. She smiles and waves, and I nod my head back at her. She's with a friend this time, and when I nodded my head, they both started to giggle.

"Why is she always here?" I ask.

"I don't know, but go and talk to her, man," Andrew encourages me.

"Nah." I shake my head.

"Jeez, Tyler, I'm not telling you to marry the girl, I'm just saying go and talk to her.

What's the worst that could happen?"

"Okay, okay, fine, I will." I throw the football back to him and jog over to the girl.

"Hey!" she says excitedly.

"Hey, what are you doing here on the football field?" I ask her.

"I like to come here every Saturday and run the track. I mean, I've been getting a little distracted ever since you started coming. I'm Carly, and this is Sabrina," she says, putting out her hand.

"Tyler, nice to meet you both," I say shaking her hand. "So, do you go to school here?"

"Um, yup. I'm in your anatomy class, actually. And your math class. And your English class," she informs me. I seriously want to punch myself right now.

"Oh god, I'm sorry," is all I manage to say.

"It's fine. I'm usually the one that sits in the back." She shrugs.

"Ah, gotcha. So, would you two like to come join us?" I offer.

"It's okay. I don't play football, and I wouldn't want to intrude," she says.

"No, c'mon, you won't. It'll be fun," I tell her.

"Alright, I'll attempt to throw a football, but I can't make any promises."

"Hey guys, they're joining us!" I yell to my friends.

"Well get your butts over here so we can play!" Andrew calls back.

CHAPTER 13

LEXI

My mom grounded me for not wanting to go to Harvard. My dad and her had this huge fight, but in the end my mom won. She always wins, and I'm sick of it. She took my phone away and I'm only allowed to use my computer for schoolwork. I'm not allowed to leave the house for a week unless I'm going to school. The whole thing is crazy. My mother is basically forcing me to attend Harvard, but honestly, I'm turning 18 soon. I'm going to be an adult, which means she can't tell me what to do anymore. Our house phone rings, making me jump. I look up from my textbook and tuck my hair behind my ears. Hmm... My mom and dad both are out shopping for furniture, so I quickly run to the phone and pick it up.

"Hello?" I ask through the phone.

"Lexi? Oh, thank god it's you. I was worried mom or dad were going to pick up. I wanted to talk to you."

"Oh my god, Amelia, you have no idea what I've been through. Mom is tearing up a storm," I tell her.

"I'm not calling to agree with you. I'm calling because I wanted to say that mom's not wrong here," she says.

I roll my eyes. "She grounded me because I don't want to go to Harvard. How can you tell me that's not wrong?" I ask.

"Well you have to understand it from her point of view. She's just upset. For twelve years all you wanted to do was go to Harvard. She did everything in her power to try and help you, and you drop a bomb on her." I get very angry at her, and before I know what's happening, I start yelling at her.

"I only said I wanted to go to Harvard because mom put so much pressure on me to go! Besides, I didn't just drop a bomb on her. We have been fighting for years over Harvard. Maybe if you actually asked me what I wanted to do instead of worrying about yourself, you actually would've known that I never wanted to go. Why did you even call? Was it to tell me that I'm wrong and mom's right?" I snap.

"What? No Lexi. I'm just trying to help," she says.

"Really? Because you're doing the complete opposite. Mom and dad are going to be here soon so I got to go," I say grumpily as I slam the phone down. I grab my books from the counter and storm upstairs. My family is so annoying. They only see one path. I haven't even gotten accepted into Harvard yet! What if I don't even get in? My mom would disown me.

The next day at school I'm feeling down. I feel like I have nothing. My family hates me, Tyler left me, and I have no plans for my future. Could this get any worse? As I'm walking in the hallway I trip over my own feet, hitting my head on the lockers. One of the teachers who witnessed this embarrassing moment sends me to the nurse's office. I assured her that I was fine and that I had to get to class, but she insisted I go and get it checked out. The nurse decides to send me home due to a massive headache and a big cut on my cheek. I really don't want to be leaving school, but one thing I've learned from my four years in high school is to never fight with the nurse. As I'm walking outside with an ice pack and a Dora the Explorer band aid on my face, I run into Bianca and her friend, Katie. I can tell they're trying not to laugh at the band aid currently stuck on my cheek.

"What happened? Are you okay?" Bianca asks.

"I'm fine. I just fell and hit my head on the lockers, and Mrs. Schmit is sending me home," I inform her.

"Ouch, that's gotta hurt," Katie comments.

"Yeah, no kidding. Well, I gotta go. I have to now go and explain to my mother why I had to leave school early. I'll catch you later," I say.

"Well, good luck with that. I'll see you later." Bianca gives me a hug and then they walk into the school.

CHAPTER 14

TYLER

Carly and I have been hanging out a lot lately. She's actually really cool, and she reminds me a lot of Lexi. She is always smiling and doesn't care what others think.

"C'mon, you can make it!" Carly cheers me on. I look at her and smile, then shoot my shot. The basketball goes right in the basket.

"Yes!" Carly jumps up and down. She laughs then runs and jumps into my arms.

"I couldn't have done it without your amazing cheerleading skills," I tease her.

"Well, I am a cheerleader, so…" she says.

"A really good one," I compliment her.

"Aw thanks!" She smiles.

"Hey guys," Sabrina says, walking up to us.

"Hey!" Carly responds.

"What's up, Tyler?" Sabrina says looking at me.

I shrug. "Nothing much."

"Tyler, your mom's calling," Ben says, sitting on the bench. I walk over and pick up my phone.

"What's up, mom?" I ask.

"Tyler, will your friends be joining us for dinner?" she asks.

"Hold on one sec." I take the phone off my ear. "Do you guys want to come over for dinner?"

"Sure!" Carly says.

"Yeah, whatever." Ben shrugs.

"Sabrina, wanna come?"

"Sure, thanks," she says.

I put the phone back up to my ear. "Yeah, they're coming."

"Great! I'll see you soon!" And she hangs up.

Even after everything she's been through, she still is the happiest person in the entire world. My dad left us so abruptly that my mom didn't have time to even talk to him. All we know about him is that he moved to Canada and got remarried. Apparently he now has two other daughters, Noelle and Brittney, and a dog named Boxer. He doesn't even bother to give me a phone call on my birthday. Yeah… he's a pretty terrible father. It still gives me chills just thinking about the man I once called my dad. We walk back to my house just as my mom finishes cooking the steaks.

"Hi mom," I smile as we walk inside.

"Smells good," Carly says.

"Thank you, dear. I take pride in my cooking. Come, sit. You four must be hungry," she says.

"Your mom's awesome," Ben whispers as we sit down. I nod my head. She is pretty cool, isn't she?

"So, what are everyone's plans for winter break?" my mom asks.

"I'm going to Hawaii. My friend invited me to go with her and her family," Carly informs us.

"That's sick. I'm going to Utah to snowboard," Ben says.

"Lucky, I wish I was going away. Our plan is to stay home and watch Christmas movies," I laugh.

"Actually, Tyler, that's not true," my mom says.

I flip my head up. "What are you talking about?"

"Tyler, I thought we went over this. We're going home for Christmas."

"Home, as in Massachusetts?" I gulp.

"Yes, Tyler, your grandparents still live there. Besides, we can't miss our famous Christmas Eve party. And on top of that, we might be moving to California in a few years, so this might be the last time we get to go back to Massachusetts for Christmas," my mom says.

"Wait, you're moving to California?" Carly asks, shocked.

"Oh, he didn't tell you? He got a full ride to Sacramento State, and since he's my only child, I'll probably end up moving there, too, sometime in the future," my mom tells her.

"Tyler, that's amazing!" Carly gushes.

"Thanks," I mumble.

Honestly, I can't even think straight. I'm going back home, to Massachusetts. I didn't think I would be going back anytime soon. What if I see Lexi? Are we even friends anymore? Will she talk to me? I have no idea how this is going to go

CHAPTER 15

LEXI

Bianca practically forces me out of my house and to the diner for breakfast. I was very satisfied in my pajamas on my bed watching cartoons, but Bianca loves to go out.

After our waiter came over and we ordered our food, Bianca looks at me.

"Did you see how hot he was?" she asks me.

"Who?" I ask, sipping on my coffee.

"The waiter! He looks like he's 19 or 20. He is so hot," she says again.

I shake my head. "Eh, he's not really my type."

"No one is your type, except Tyler." She raises her eyebrows. I can feel my cheeks go red. Of course Tyler is the only person that's my type. He was the best thing that ever happened to me.

"What? That is not true," I lie.

"Fine, then go and ask that guy for his number," she says, looking in his direction.

"No way."

"Because you still love Tyler," she says.

"No, I don't."

"Yes you do."

"No, I don't," I repeat myself.

"Lexi, why are you having a tough time admitting it? You still love him, and you still want to be with him. You're blushing just thinking about him."

"Bianca—"

"You guys can make this long distance relationship work. I know you can, and Tyler knows you can. You're the only one that doesn't think so."

"Okay, fine, I still love Tyler. But it doesn't matter anymore. We're over," I say.

"Lexi, go get him."

"What?"

"You heard me."

"Bianca, I can't just go to Connecticut," I say to her.

"Yes, you can. C'mon, live a little. Break some rules. Have some fun. It's only a couple hours away," she says.

"You really think I should go?" I ask her.

"Yes! Go, now! I'll stay and get this waiter's number." I grab my purse and jump out of the booth.

"You know what, you're right. Thanks, Bianca."

"Anything for you. Now go get your man back!"

CHAPTER 16

TYLER

"What did you get for number five?" I ask Carly.

"Twenty-seven," she replies.

"I don't wanna do math anymore. My head's hurting," I groan, throwing my books to the side.

"Well, we can take a break. Where's your bathroom?"

"Down the hall, to the right," I reply.

"I'll be right back," she gets up from off the couch and skips to the bathroom. I grab the remote and flip through the channels on the TV when there's a knock on the door. I place the remote on the small wooden table next to the couch. I walk over to the door and swing it open.

"Hi, Tyler," Lexi says, smiling. My eyes go wide. I must be imagining things. There is no way Lexi can be really here, on my porch.

"Tyler," Lexi waves her hand in front of my face.

"You're here," I manage to say.

"Yes, I'm really here. So are you going to let me in, or am I going to have to freeze my butt off out here?" Lexi says.

"Tyler, who's at the door?" Carly says appearing at my side. Lexi looks at her, then back at me.

"Oh, I didn't know you had company. I'll show myself out," Lexi says, turning around.

"No, wait, Lexi. You can stay. I want you to," I tell her.

"No, it's okay. This clearly was a mistake. You two can go back to whatever you guys were doing," Lexi says. Oh god, she thinks that Carly is my girlfriend.

"Hi, I'm Carly," Carly says with a smile.

"I really don't care," Lexi snaps.

"Look, this obviously is a big misunderstanding. Lexi, Carly is just a friend," I say to her.

"That's how we started out, Tyler, as just friends," Lexi says, crossing her arms.

"Please don't get angry about this. You broke up with me, remember?" I point out.

"I get it, okay? You moved on with your life. You have a new house, a new school, new friends, and soon a new girlfriend. It's good that you're not holding onto your past." Man she's pissed. I can read Lexi like a book. She's just trying to hold it together.

"But that's the thing, Lexi. I haven't moved on with my life. I still want to be with you. And since you drove all the way out here, I'm pretty sure you feel the same way."

Lexi's phone starts ringing. She digs through her purse and takes it out.

62

"It's my mom. She's probably freaking out right now. I really have to go," Lexi says before answering it. I can hear her mom yelling through the speaker.

"I'm okay, mom, I'll be home in a couple of hours." She turns around and starts walking to the car. After she hangs up, she opens the car door and looks at me.

"I really do hope you have a nice life, Tyler."

"Lexi, please don't leave me again," I beg.

"I'm sorry," she mumbles before getting in the car. I watch as she drives down my street and turns the corner. She's gone. I look back at Carly.

"And when were you planning on telling me about her?" Carly asks, raising her eyebrows.

"I just didn't want to talk about it," I tell her.

"Hey guys, sorry I'm late," Sabrina says as she makes her way up the porch.

"You invited Sabrina?" I mouth to Carly. She shrugs and replies with a simple yes.

"Are you two okay? Did I miss something?" Sabrina asks.

"Tyler's crazy ex-girlfriend just showed up out of nowhere then left after she saw me. It was weird," Carly explains.

"She's not crazy," I defend her.

"Oh, well I think that any girl is lucky to have you and it's her loss. Anyways, can we get started on the homework?" Sabrina asks.

CHAPTER 17

LEXI

"What were you thinking? You drove all the way to Connecticut without telling me? We were worried sick!" my mom yells at me.

I'm again sitting on the couch, watching my mom's face turn red. She is so mad at me, but then again I'm used to this reaction from my mother. In her eyes, everything I do is wrong.

"I'm sorry mom, okay? I just needed to see him. I promise it won't happen again,"

I say.

"You're darn right it won't happen again. You live under my roof, and it's my rules you have to follow. I will not have another conversation about this young lady!"

"Ok I get it. Can I go now?" I ask, extremely annoyed by this whole situation.

"This is serious, Alexa! Telling me you don't want to go to Harvard is one thing, but going to a different state without telling me is another! I can't trust you," she says.

"Oh, please, you've never trusted me," I fight back.

"You're right, I never have. You're grounded for another three weeks. Wash up before dinner. Go," she waves me off and walks back in the kitchen.

I go back to my room and sit on my bed. I can't believe I drove all the way to Connecticut just to see Tyler with another girl. Just two weeks ago he came to my school to beat up a guy that made me look like a fool. Ugh! He makes me so mad! I just don't get it. I look to the side of my bed and pick up the picture of us on our first date. We looked so happy, young, naive – well, good thing I grew up. I throw the picture in the trash, shattering the glass in a million little pieces, just like my heart.

The next day at school Bianca asks me questions non-stop, but I don't feel like talking about what happened in Connecticut. I'm still so embarrassed. I should've known that he would've moved on. I can't be the only girl he's attracted to, and believe me, that girl he was with is beautiful. I grab my history book and shut my locker.

"Look, nothing happened. When I got to his house, his mom said that he went out for the weekend to some guy's beach house in New Jersey," I lie.

"So? Why couldn't you wait for him?" she asks me.

"Because I had to get back home," I answer.

"Excuse me, ladies, but do you know where classroom three-zero-one is? I'm supposed to be there in exactly two minutes, and I have no idea where I'm going," a boy interrupts our conversation. I secretly thank him in my head for distracting Bianca from asking me any more questions.

"Do we know you?" she asks.

"No, I just transferred here from Alabama. My name is James," he introduces himself.

"Oh, well my name is Bianca, and this is my friend Lexi."

"I'm in that class. You can come with me. Bye, Bianca, see you at lunch," I say.

As I walk away, I hear James saying bye to her, then he follows me.

"So, why did you move?" I ask curiously.

"My parents just got a divorce, and my mom decided to move back to Massachusetts where her family lives."

"Oh, I'm sorry. That must be tough moving in the middle of the school year," I say.

"Yeah, it is." After a moment of awkward silence, he starts talking again.

"So, is every girl here as cute as you?" he asks. I stop dead in my tracks and look at him.

"What are you doing?" I ask him.

"Just trying to be friendly, that's all," he says.

★ ★ ★

"James is so hot," Bianca gushes at lunch. I take a bite out of my cheese sandwich and look at her.

"Yeah, I guess." I shrug.

"Finally, you admit that another boy other than Tyler is hot," she says.

"He called me cute today," I admit.

Her mouth drops open. "Oh my god, you should totally go for him."

"Bianca, I just met him today. Besides, I don't think I'm ready to date yet."

"You do whatever you want. All I'm saying is that you should consider James as an option," she says before shoving another bite of pizza in her mouth.

"Hey, ladies. Mind if I join you?" James asks us.

"Sure! No problem." Bianca smiles. James takes a seat in front of us and starts putting dressing on his salad.

"I don't mean to intrude on your conversation, but you two are the only ones I've met so far, and I don't want to sit alone," James explains.

"It's totally fine, we don't mind," I say. Bianca looks at me out of the corner of her eye, making me smile. I know exactly what she's thinking. She has been trying to help me find a guy ever since Tyler left, and she thinks this is the perfect opportunity for me to start dating again. So I do what I do best and avoid the situation.

"I have to use the restroom," I quickly say.

"What? Can't you hold it until after lunch?" Bianca asks.

"Sorry, I really have to go. I'm probably going to just head straight to class afterwards because lunch is almost over. I'll see you around," I say.

I grab my backpack, fling it over my shoulder, and hurry out of the cafeteria. I head straight towards the bathroom and hide in a stall. I just needed some space from Bianca and James. It's like all I'm ever talking about these days are boys. I just need the drama to stop. I'm Lexi Marget, for crying out loud. My sole focus should be on school.

If my mother knew what was going on in my head half the time, she would be livid.

* * *

The next day I grab my books out of my locker and slip them in my backpack. I swing it over my shoulder and begin walking to my Chinese honors class, without a doubt, my favorite class. The fact that I get to transport myself into another culture through language is such a beautiful thing. When done with college, I plan on going to China for at least two months to reward myself. I can speak the language well, and I think it will be good for myself to be on my own. I was planning on having Tyler come with me, but that obviously is not going to happen.

"Hey," James says from behind me. I turn my head and look at him. His wavy brown hair is escaping out from under his baseball cap.

"Hey," I say back.

"What's up?" he asks.

"Nothing much," I say, shrugging.

"So, listen, I hope I didn't scare you off yesterday. If I did, I'm sorry," he says.

"No, you didn't. I'm sorry I made you feel that way. Truth is, I think you're a really nice guy."

"So, maybe we could try to be friends? It's tough being the new kid, and I would love it if you would be my first real friend," he admits. I smile.

"I'll absolutely be your first real friend. And I'm sure Bianca will be your friend, as well. So now you have two real friends."

"You're pretty awesome, you know that?"

"I know. I gotta get to class, but I'll see you later," I say before emphasizing, "friend."

* * *

James and I actually have gotten really close. He's a chill person and fun to be around. There's never a dull moment when I'm with him. We have spent the last couple of weeks getting to know each other and just hanging out. I can't help but think maybe I'm starting to fall for him. He's got every quality I look for in a guy, and I love spending time with him. As I'm sitting on my bed writing an equation for math, my phone rings. I smile when I see his name light up on my phone. "James, what's up?" I ask when I answer.

"My mom is having a couple of old friends over tonight, so I was wondering if maybe I could come over and escape the mayhem at my place?" he asks me.

"Yeah, sure, my parents aren't supposed to be home for another couple hours," I say to him.

"Cool, I'll see you soon."

I quickly run to the bathroom and grab the straight iron. I shouldn't care so much about what I look like when I'm with James, but I can't help it. There's something about being with him that makes me happy. The doorbell rings just as I finish my hair. I skip downstairs and swing the door open.

"Hey, Lexi," James says with a smile as he walks in.

"Hey," I say, shutting the door behind him.

"You look nice." He smiles before walking over to the couch and sitting down.

Just hearing him say that makes me blush. What is happening to me? The only other time I've felt like this before was the first time Tyler and I hung out.

"So, are you going to just stand there or sit next to me?" James asks. I realize I haven't moved from my spot since he walked in. I smile and make my way over to the couch.

"Wanna watch some TV?" I offer.

"Sure.".

I grab the remote and flick through the channels until we both can agree on a movie to watch. Have I finally gotten over Tyler? I never thought in a million years that would be possible. As we're watching the movie, our hands accidentally touch. I quickly pull my hand away.

"Sorry," I mutter. He looks at me.

"You don't have to be sorry." He grabs my hand and places it in his. He lays our hands on the couch and continues watching the movie. My heart speeds up as I feel his rough hand against mine.

"Lexi?" James says. I look at him.

"Yeah?" I ask. We lock eyes and he smiles.

"I'm glad I wasn't the only one feeling the connection." I smile and look down.

"Me, too," I say quietly. He brings his head closer to mine.

"You never have to be shy around me," he says, lifting my head up until we're inches away from each other. I stare into his beautiful brown eyes as he looks into mine.

"Are you going to kiss me now?" I ask him. He nods his head.

"That's the only reason I came over here," he says before his lips come crashing down on mine.

I pull back. "Wait, so your mom never was going to have any friends over?"

He bites his bottom lip and shakes his head. "Nope, I made it all up," he says before grabbing my head and kissing me again.

* * *

A month has passed, and I finally feel like I have gotten over Tyler. I have a boyfriend I have been dating for a couple of weeks now, and I'm really happy. I thought after I completely embarrassed myself in Connecticut I would never find someone like Tyler, and I still haven't. But I've got the next best thing.

Christmas is my favorite time of year. I love getting a Christmas tree, listening to carols, and looking at the beautiful lights. And who can forget winter break? I basically drag my boyfriend to the mall to help me pick out a gift for my mom, dad, Amelia, and Bianca.

"Can't we just go to the dollar store?" James complains. I laugh.

"Do I look like the type of person that's cheap?" I raise my eyebrows.

"Definitely not."

"Okay. So my mom for whatever reason loves candles. Come with me," I grab his hand and we walk into the store. We head over to the candle section, and I pick up an apple cinnamon scent. I twist the lid off and give it a sniff. Oh god, that smells terrible. I quickly put it back and pick up another one. After finding no candles that smell nice, James calls me over.

"Babe, smell this one."

"Babe?" someone behind me says. I turn around, then almost drop the candle I'm holding. It's Tyler.

"What are you doing here?" I ask him.

"My mom needed a new comforter," Tyler says. James appears at my side in a second and wraps his arm around me.

"I'm James, Lexi's boyfriend," he introduces himself. Tyler looks at me, then back at James.

"I'm Tyler, Lexi's ex-boyfriend," he says.

"Oh, so you're the one who dumped her on her ass for Connecticut," James smirks.

"Okay, I think it's time to go," I laugh nervously.

"No wait, hold on. I may have moved to Connecticut, but don't think for a second that I wouldn't rather be here with her. So get off your high horse because believe me, she feels the same way," Tyler snaps. I blink. What was that? What do I do? I have two boys staring at me waiting for a response, and I got nothing.

"I, um … I," I mumble.

"It's okay, babe, I think it's time for us to go," James says before kissing my cheek.

"It was nice seeing you again, Tyler," I tell him. James grabs my hand and we walk past him.

When I get home I see another car in the driveway. That's strange. I unlock the door and walk inside.

"Alexa, come here please," my mom calls from the living room. I walk in and see her sitting on the couch, then I turn my head and see the most unexpected guest sitting next to her.

"Oh, Lexi!" Tyler's mom exclaims. She throws her arms around me and gives me the biggest hug. What is she doing in our house?

"Hi! How are you?" I ask her.

"I'm fabulous, and you?" she asks me.

"I'm okay, is that a new car?" I ask her. She used to have a red Chevrolet, but the car in my driveway was a white Volvo.

"I'm glad you noticed! I got it in right before we left Connecticut. Do you like it?"

"It's great," I look at my mom, waiting for her to explain what is happening. We never have company over, because everyone is scared of my mom. Even I'm scared of my mom!

"Linda stopped by to have a chat. She invited us over for her Christmas Eve party she's having, and I accepted the invitation. Isn't it wonderful?" my mom tells me.

She did what?

"Mom, don't you think that would be a little uncomfortable considering we aren't together anymore?" I ask her.

"You drove to Connecticut just to see him. I don't think it would hurt to go to a party he'll be at," she says in a stern voice. I get it now. This is her way of punishing me for going to Connecticut.

"Lexi, darling, I can see how this might be a little awkward for both of you, but I would love it if you guys could come. I'm sure once I tell him he'll be very excited to see you," she says while squeezing my hand.

"We'll be there," my mom ensures her.

CHAPTER 18

TYLER

"Are you out of your damn mind!" I yell at my mom.

"Tyler calm down. I just invited them to a party, that's all," she says.

"You invited my ex-girlfriend to a party we're hosting and didn't even bother to tell me! And I'm supposed to be calm?"

"It was the right thing to do. Lexi came every year, and I thought it was time her parents came this time," she says.

"Mom, she hates me. This is going to be so awkward."

"It's only going to be awkward if you make it awkward," she points out.

"Tyler, please don't be mad at your mother. She was only trying to help," my grandmother intervenes.

I groan and march to my room. She barely even looked at me at the mall today. I mean, she has a boyfriend and didn't even tell me about him. I guess I deserve it. I didn't tell her about Carly. I didn't even tell Carly about Lexi, either. In a way, I'm happy Lexi got over what happened back in Connecticut. I was worried that she was still going to be devastated, and I don't want her to feel like that, especially because of me. I just wished she hadn't moved on to another dude. Now she's going to actually be inside my house for the first time in months. Thank god other people are going to be there. I have to try and talk to her. I have to tell her that nothing has happened between me and Carly. She has to understand that I'm still crazy about her.

* * *

My mom and grandma decide to go to lunch, so I'm by myself. Apparently I'm not allowed on school grounds anymore, or else I would pop in and say hello. I played video games, watched TV, and heated up some frozen pizza for myself. As I'm eating the pizza, I hear the door open in close.

"Mom?" I ask. No answer. I put the pizza down and stand up. "Hello?" I ask again before slowly walking towards the door. Just then, someone jumps right in front of me and screams, "Boo!" I jump so high and almost have a heart attack.

"Carl! Not funny. I almost called the cops!" I punch him in the arm.

"Sorry, Ty, but the door was unlocked."

"I hate you," I say while walking back to the counter to finish my pizza.

"Please, you love me," he says.

'Where's Aunt Carmine and Uncle Danny?" I ask him.

"They're coming later tonight. I'm pretty sure Aunt Steph and

Uncle Steve are coming tomorrow morning with Nikki and Lena," Carl informs me. Steph and Carmine are my mom's sisters, and Carl, Nikki, and Lena are my cousins. Nikki and Lena are younger, 12 and 8. We always celebrate Christmas together, and they always come to our Christmas Eve party. Which means they all know Lexi.

"I can't wait for another one of your epic Christmas Eve parties tomorrow," Carl says, lying on the couch.

"Yeah, well I just want it to be over with," I grumble.

"Why?" Carl asks, flicking through the channels on the TV.

"Well, funny you ask that. My mom took it upon herself to invite Lexi and her whole family to our epic Christmas Eve party," I explain.

"Sheesh, that's going to be awkward. Do you know if Amelia's going to be there?" Carl asks.

"She is home from college, so I would think so. Do you still have a thing for her?" I raise my eyebrows.

"What? No. Shut up." Carl's face turns red. I love embarrassing him. Carl has had a thing for Amelia ever since he came with me to pick up Lexi and Amelia to go to this water park that Lexi loves. Lexi and I had just started dating, so of course we did everything together, leaving Amelia and Carl by themselves. He has had a big fat crush on her ever since.

CHAPTER 19

LEXI

I just finished baking brownies for this stupid party I'm being forced to go to. As I'm putting the supplies away, Amelia walks into the kitchen.

"Can I just say, I love the pink in your hair," she says.

"Not everyone feels the same way," I reply.

"Mom wanted me to tell you to get dressed. We're leaving in half an hour. She also wanted me to tell you to dress nice," she adds before walking away. I roll my eyes and head to my room. After searching through my closet, I find a gorgeous white dress with matching heels. I only wore this dress once, and that was to Bianca's seventeenth birthday party. As I slip the dress on, a part of me can't help but wonder if Tyler is going to like it. I know I still shouldn't be trying to impress him, but I can't help it. Tyler was the first boy that ever made me feel beautiful and loved. No Lexi, stop it. You're with James now. I shake the thought of Tyler out of my head and look in the mirror.

"Alexa, let's go!" my mom yells from downstairs. I roll my eyes. She refuses to call me Lexi. She said it sounds immature and that my real name is Alexa. It's beyond annoying.

As we're driving to Tyler's house, my heart starts beating fast. I don't know why I'm so nervous. Maybe it's because I'll be surrounded by Tyler's family. Do they know we broke up? What if they hate me? We get to his house and my mom rings the doorbell, and we are greeted at the door by Carl.

"Hi guys! Come on in." Carl smiles. He passes me and instantly hugs Amelia.

What's that all about?

"Lexi! Lexi!" Lena screams while running up to me. She runs into my arms and I pick her up.

"I missed you," I say to the little girl.

"I missed you, too! Guess what!" she says excitedly.

"What?"

"Mommy taught me how to ride a bike!"

"No way," I say.

"Wanna play pretty princesses with me?"

"Of course." As we walk through the house and into the backyard, I spot Tyler talking to his uncle. I watch as he brushes his hand through his brown hair, and I can't help but stare. He has his back against the wall, laughing at something his uncle has said.

"Lexi!" Mrs. McHale says a little too loud as she gives me a hug. Tyler looks past his uncle and directly at me. His mouth parts slightly as we lock eyes. I quickly turn my back to him and look at his mom.

"Hi, Mrs. McHale." I attempt to smile.

"I'm so glad you were able to make it. Well, I don't want to keep you from playing with Lena. I'll see you a little later." She nods her head and walks to the group of adults standing around the kitchen table.

"Are you ready to play?" I ask as excitedly as I can to Lena. I really do not want to be here right now, but it's like my mother always says: fake it till you make it.

After about half an hour of playing with Lena, I need water. I head into the kitchen and grab a water bottle from the fridge when I hear my name being called. I turn around and smile.

"Hey, Carl, what's up?" I ask, putting the bottle to my mouth.

"Do you know where Amelia is? I've been looking for her everywhere," he asks.

"No, I don't. Maybe she's upstairs?" My phone starts ringing. It's James.

"I gotta take this, sorry I couldn't be much help," I say. I put the phone to my ear and walk outside.

"Hey," I say, taking a seat on the steps.

"Hey, whatcha doing?" he asks me.

"I'm heading over to Bianca's now for that Christmas Eve's Party," I lie.

"Oh, right, I forgot. Tell Bianca I said hi," he says.

"Will do."

"I'm pretty sure Bianca wasn't invited," someone behind me says. I whip my head around.

"Lexi? You still there?" James asks through the phone.

"Uh, I gotta go. We're about to eat dinner," I mumble and

quickly hang up the phone.

"Lying to your new boyfriend already?" Tyler smirks, standing in the doorway. He sits next to me.

"He would flip if he knew I was at your house. Besides, you shouldn't give me a lecture about lying. You've been doing it for months," I snap.

"How many times do I have to apologize to you? Lexi, I'm sorry," Tyler says.

"Don't you get it, Tyler? If you had just told me you were moving in the first place, I would've stuck by you. You should know that by now. I almost ruined my relationship with my own mother for you!" I throw my hands up in the air. Tyler rubs his hand over his face.

"I know that. I think about what I did to you every day, and I regret it more than you'll ever know."

"Good, you should. It doesn't matter now, anyways. I'm happy with James."

"Right. James," Tyler mumbles.

We sit there in silence for about a minute, just staring at the road ahead of us. Tyler really hurt me, but just sitting next to him gives me chills. No matter how much I try to forget about him, that beautiful smile of his just comes floating right back in my mind. He shouldn't have this much control over me, especially since I'm with James now, but unfortunately he does.

"Do you hate me?" he finally asks.

"I don't think I could ever hate you," I answer honestly.

"Good."

All of a sudden he grabs my face and his lips come crashing down on mine.

CHAPTER 20

TYLER

I can't believe I just did that. If Lexi didn't hate me then, she definitely hates me now. What was I thinking? She has a boyfriend! I gotta admit, it was a pretty good kiss.

Well, it was good for about ten seconds, until she ran away. I wasn't planning on doing that. I was planning on having a mature conversation with her. But just sitting next to Lexi made all of those feelings I had for her come back and I couldn't help myself.

I throw myself on my bed and cover my face in my pillow. I am so stupid. I hear a knock on my door and the stupid squeaking sound that my door makes when it opens.

My dad promised my grandparents that he would fix it, but he left before he got the

chance.

"Sweetie, I brought up some chocolate cake. You didn't eat much at the dinner party," my mom says, sitting on the corner of my bed.

"Yeah, because I'm not hungry," I tell her. I sit up and stare at the wall.

"Tyler, is everything okay? Is this about Lexi leaving early? Because honey, if it is, she wasn't feeling well. There's nothing you can do about that," my mom says while rubbing my back.

"Everything's fine mom. Did everyone leave yet?" I ask.

"Yes, they all left around eight." Just then we hear a knock on the door.

"I got it," I grumble. I get up from my bed and make my way downstairs. I quickly open the door, ready to tell whoever was on the porch to leave.

"What?" I say grumpily. I stop myself as I stare at the girl in front of me.

"Carly?" My eyes go wide.

"Surprise!" she says, jumping into my arms.

"What are you doing here?" I ask her.

"I thought I should come and check out your home town. Besides, my friend canceled our Hawaii vacation. She apparently got the flu. Oh, and here! Merry Christmas!" She hands me a perfectly wrapped Christmas present.

"Carly, I'm so glad you could make it," my mom says, coming down the stairs. I look at my mom.

"You knew about this?" I ask her.

"Of course I did. How do you think she knows where your grandparents live?" My mom chuckles.

"I have to go and help my mom unpack in the hotel, but I just wanted to say a quick hello. I'll see you later, alright?" Carly says.

"Yeah, of course. I'll see you," I say before shutting the door. I look at my mom and raise my eyebrows.

"What? I thought you could use a friend." She shrugs before walking back upstairs.

* * *

I wake up to the smell of freshly baked cookies. What is my mom doing at eight in the morning? I stand up and stretch my arms out. I make my way downstairs where my mom greets me with a smile as she puts the finishing touches on our pancakes. I look at my plate and laugh. She made a smiley face on the pancakes with whipped cream and blueberries.

"Really, mom?" I laugh.

"What? You used to love this as a kid. It's tradition," she says to me. I put a blueberry in my mouth and look at her.

"What are you doing?" I ask. My eyes shift to the newly baked chocolate chip cookies sitting on the counter.

"Oh, your grandmother asked me to make treats for tonight," she explains as she wipes her hands on her apron.

"Where is grandma and grandpa, anyway?"

"They forgot a few ingredients for their coq au vin rosé," she says with an accent.

I smile and take another bite out of my pancakes.

"Don't worry, though, they'll be back soon. Then after we can open gifts. Oh, and by the way, Merry Christmas!" she says, giving me a hug.

"Merry Christmas, mom," I say, hugging her back.

CHAPTER 21

LEXI

"Alexa, this one's for you," my mom says, handing me a present.

I open it up, then my smile disappears. It's a Harvard t-shirt. I want to explode, but instead I look at her.

"Awesome, thanks, mom," I say through gritted teeth.

"Okay, well I think that's the last present, so who's hungry? I made ham and mashed potatoes for lunch," my mom says.

"C'mon girls, let's eat," my dad says to us.

"This is very good, mom," Amelia says to her. I roll my eyes. Amelia is such a kiss ass. No wonder why mom loves her more than me.

"Thank you, Amelia. What do you think, Alexa?" my mom asks me.

"About what? About the fact that you gave me a Harvard shirt or the food?" I snap. Wow, I really can't control myself anymore. Maybe Tyler is a bad influence on me.

He's gotten into more fights than I can count. It probably rubbed off on me.

"Alexa, we are not having another conversation about this. So drop it," she says while cutting into her food.

"I should probably give the shirt to Julian Thobbs. You know, the kid in my grade that actually really wants to go to Harvard. He probably needs it more than me," I say. She puts her fork down and looks at me.

"I thought we agreed that you would go to Harvard," she says angrily.

"No, you decided, I just listened. You didn't even give me a chance to talk," I tell her.

"Okay, c'mon you two. It's Christmas. Let's enjoy today, please," Amelia begs.

"Yes, I agree. Today is about family," my dad says.

"Family? What family?" I mumble.

"What did you say?" my mom asks.

"Nothing," I say as I put ham in my mouth. I can feel fumes coming out of my ears, but I am not going to be the one to ruin Christmas. It's my favorite time of year, and I refuse to let my mother destroy it for me, just like she does with everything else.

* * *

"Is everything all right?" James asks as soon as he picks up the phone.

"My mother is driving me insane," I inform him.

"That's a mother's job," James jokes.

"I'm serious, James. We had another fight about Harvard."

"Don't worry about it, babe. How about tomorrow we hang out? We can go to the park," he offers.

"That is just what I need."

"Great, see you tomorrow. Enjoy today. Oh, and Merry Christmas," he says.

"I'll try, see you tomorrow. Merry Christmas," I say before hanging up the phone.

The next day I get ready to meet James. I really need this day to relax and forget about my mom and Harvard.

"Amelia, tell mom and dad I'm leaving," I say to her as I walk out the door. I drive to the park and search for James. All of a sudden someone comes up from behind me and touches my back, making me jump. I turn around hesitantly.

"James!" I exclaim. He laughs then hugs me.

"Come with me." He takes my hand and walks me over to a bench. We both sit and he puts his arm around me.

"I know we said we wouldn't get each other gifts, but I just couldn't help it." He takes out a small box from his pocket and hands it to me.

"Aw, James," I say, smiling. I open the box. It's a pair of beautiful silver earrings. I pointed these out to him at the mall one day, and I can't believe he remembered.

"Oh my god, James! I can't believe this. Thank you so much," I gush.

"I knew you would like them." I place my head on his shoulder and enjoy the view. For a minute silence surrounds us, and we just take in the beautiful sight in front of us. I remember coming here when I was little. There was something about this place that made me just relax. Amelia and I would run around and climb up trees like there was no tomorrow. My mom always got mad at us. Her exact words were, "Girls who climb up trees and play tag are immature." I cringe at the thought of my mom, who single-handedly took away my childhood.

"Do you want to go to dinner tonight?" James asks me as he strokes my arm.

"Sure, where would you like to go?"

"My cousin told me about some great Italian place right outside of town. It's right on the water, and apparently their food is amazing," James says.

"That sounds fantastic."

"Yeah, well I know how much you like the view, so I'll make sure to get us a table right on the water," he says, kissing my forehead. I look at him and smile.

"How did I get so lucky?"

"I am a pretty great guy, aren't I?" he jokes. I chuckle and rest my head back down.

"You really are."

James really is a good guy, which is why I feel so guilty thinking about Tyler. He lied to me and hurt me, yet I can't get him out of my mind. That kiss we shared was something special. Even though I ran away, I really didn't want to leave. Does that make me a bad person? I don't know. What I do know is that James cares about me, and he loves me. I can't just leave him for a boy who broke my heart. It wouldn't be right.

"Hey, Amelia," I say, walking through the door.

"Hey," she says as she continues to scribble something on her paper.

"Whatcha working on?" I ask her.

"I'm distracting myself. I need your advice," she says putting down her pencil.

"Okay, what's up?" I ask as I grab a banana.

"Carl asked me out to dinner," she says. I take a bite out of my banana and wait for her to continue, but she doesn't.

"Okay? And what's the problem?" I ask.

"Well, what if I embarrass myself? You know when I'm nervous I start to say the weirdest things," she explains. I raise my eyebrows.

"So you do like him?"

"What? No." I notice her cheeks turning the color pink as she tries to deny it.

"Whatever, Amelia you're going to be fine," I reassure her.

"No. I'm not. I can't do this. I'm going to call him right now and cancel," she starts to freak out.

"Wait! Stop. I have a solution. Come with me and James tomorrow out to dinner.

Tell Carl that we're going on a double date," I say.

"James will be okay with that?" she asks.

"Yeah, totally ..."

* * *

"No, absolutely not," James says through the phone.

"C'mon James, she's my sister and she needs our help. I promise it will be just this once."

"The reservation is only for two," he argues.

"Well, call and tell them it's for four," I answer. I hear him sigh.

"Fine, we'll help your sister, but just this once," he gives in.

"Thank you so much. Got to go, love you," I say.

"Love you too."

I hang up my phone and throw it on the bed. I sit in a chair and stare at the window. Tyler kissed me. I mean, he really kissed me. Am I supposed to just forget about it and move on with James? That's probably what I should do. But why am I having a tough time doing it? And why am I even thinking about Tyler? He lied to me. A relationship is built on trust, and right now, I don't trust Tyler.

CHAPTER 22

TYLER

I wake up to the sound of my ringtone going off. I rub my hand over my face then grab my phone off of the nightstand next to my bed.

"Hello?" I grumble.

"Good, you're awake. Wanna go and get some breakfast?" Carly asks.

"How do you have this much energy at seven thirty in the morning?"

"I'm an early riser. C'mon, get dressed and I'll be at your house in half an hour."

"Well someone has their bossy pants on," I tease.

"Bye," she breathes out before hanging up. I stand up and stretch my arms out. I make my way downstairs to find my grandfather sitting on the couch, reading the newspaper.

"Hi pops," I say, sitting next to him.

"Boy! They write the same damn thing in this newspaper every morning. How else am I supposed to get the news?" he says out of frustration.

"Maybe you could try turning on the TV and watching the news there," I suggest.

"You know, when I was growing up, my family didn't even bother to buy a TV.

Why should I start watching it now?"

"I'm going out to breakfast with a friend soon, but I just wanted to say a quick hello," I say.

"Is it Lexi? I always loved that girl. Give her my best will you?"

I look down on the ground. "Grandpa, remember? I told you that Lexi and I broke up."

"Oh, you did? I'm so sorry. You want to talk about it?" Grandpa asks.

"No, it's okay, but I appreciate it."

"Okay, well I better get back to reading. Carmine, bring me my reading glasses!" he shouts to my grandmother. I nod my head and stand up.

I love my grandpa, I really do, but he's getting old, and it's hard to see him this way. He's very forgetful and my mom is starting to talk about putting him in a nursing home. Of course my grandmother is very opposed to it, but eventually it's what has to be done. I walk upstairs and throw on a black t-shirt and jeans, then grab my black leather jacket. I brush my teeth and then run into my mom in the hallway.

"Well, good morning. Where are you heading off to?" she asks me.

"I'm going to grab some breakfast with Carly. Is that okay?" I ask.

"Of course it is. Have fun," she says, smiling.

"Do you want me to bring anything back for you?" I offer.

"Can you just bring back two breakfast sandwiches for your grandparents? One with egg and sausage and the other with egg, sausage, and cheese," she says. Just then the doorbell rings.

"Will do. Gotta go. Love you," I say before heading downstairs. I open the door.

"Hey," Carly says with a big smile.

"You ready to go? There's a French bakery on the next street over. I used to go there all the time with—" I stop myself. Why does every memory have to involve Lexi?

"Alright then, let's go," Carly says, trying not to laugh at me. I put the car in reverse and back out of the driveway.

"I still can't believe you're here," I comment as I stare at the road in front of me.

"Why? We are friends, aren't we?"

"Well yeah, you're one of my closest friends. To be honest, I'm actually relieved you're here. I could really use someone like you after what happened on Christmas Eve," I say.

"What are you talking about?"

"I kissed Lexi," I tell her.

Carly gasps. "You did what?"

"You heard me."

"Well did she kiss you back?" Carly asks.

"She ran away," I answer Carly puts her palm to her forehead.

"That is the worst response to a kiss that I've ever heard."

"Wow Carly, thanks for your help. You really made me feel better," I say sarcastically. I pull into the parking lot and park. "Let's just drop it, ok? I want to have fun today and not even think about Lexi," I state, getting out of the car.

"Deal," I hear Carly reply.

I open the rustic brown door for Carly, allowing her to walk inside the small bakery.

"This place smells so good," Carly says. I nod my head in agreement and we walk up to the counter.

"Excuse me," I say to the guy, who has his back turned to us. He turns around and smiles.

"No fricken way. Tyler McHale, what's up man?" Connor says, leaning against the counter. Connor and I had played football together. He was the wide receiver and was pretty damn good. We were pals all the way until junior year, when he met a girl who basically took him away. He quit football, stopped hanging with us, and even ditched school. I think they just broke up, so I'm sure he's regretting everything he did.

"Nothing much, just getting something to eat. You work here now?" I ask.

"Sure do, who's this? Your new girl?" Connor asks, referring to Carly.

"Oh no, we're just friends. She's from Connecticut," I explain.

"Ah, I see. Well, we all miss you around here. It definitely hasn't been the same without you."

"I miss this place, too. It's weird being back here, but I'm happy to see everyone," I say.

"And by everyone, you mean Lexi?" Connor asks, raising his eyebrows.

"Oh, shut up," I say.

"So, what would you two like to get?" Connor asks. After we place our order we sit at a table far away from the counter. I don't need creepy Connor interrupting our breakfast. It's too early in the morning to deal with him.

"Your friend's kinda cute," Carly says.

"Carly, in case you didn't know, I'm a guy. I don't look at other guys and be like,

'Oh he's cute,'" I say, mocking her.

"So, are you going to the dance?" she asks me.

"What dance?" I ask, confused.

"Oh, you don't know? Every year, our school throws a winter dance for the juniors and seniors. It's always a week after we come back from winter break. It's kinda like prom but in the winter. So, you going?"

"Not a chance," I shake my head.

"What, why?" she asks in disbelief.

"Because if I can't go with Lexi, then I don't want to go at all."

"You're unbelievable." She shakes her head.

"Dances aren't for me, anyways." I shrug, and she rolls her eyes.

"Okay, okay, fine. So, what's the plan for today?"

"What makes you think I have a plan for today?" I ask.

"C'mon, what did you do around here for fun?"

"Well, there's this awesome arcade that I went to all the time with—" I stop myself, again. This time Carly bursts out laughing while I put my palm to my forehead.

What is wrong with me?

"That sounds fun. I'm totally up to go to the arcade. What do you suggest we do for dinner?"

"You're already thinking about dinner? We haven't even eaten our breakfast yet," I point out.

"Yeah, but I like to know the plan. I was thinking maybe Italian. Are there some good Italian restaurants around here?" she asks.

"Actually, there is. My mom and I would always go there for my birthday. It's right outside of town. I should warn you, though, it's more on the fancier side," I say.

"I'm down. Oh, here comes our food," Carly says looking behind me.

After breakfast, I drop the sandwiches off at the house then take Carly to the arcade. It's very old-school and a lot of kids my age come here. It's like the place to be.

"Oh my god, they have Pac Man," Carly says, walking over to the rusty machine.

"Of course they do. What arcade doesn't?" I laugh. She slips two quarters into the slot then starts playing but loses within 20 seconds.

"This game's rigged!" She frowns.

"Or maybe you're just really bad," I say.

"Yeah, well I can beat you in air hockey." She crosses her arms.

"I'd like to see you try."

I walk over to the air hockey machine and start it up. She stands on one side while I stand on the other. Carly starts to swing her arm in a circular motion as if she's stretching out her shoulder. To be honest, she looks like she's going into battle.

"Are you ready to lose?" I ask her.

"Not a chance," she says before hitting the puck right into my goal.

Carly and I had so much fun at the arcade. After both of us won once in air hockey, we decided to call it quits. Why have only one person win when both of us could win? It's not usually my mentality. I'm actually a very competitive person, but it was Carly's idea and so I went along with it. She has to head back to the hotel to get ready for dinner, so I go home and find my mom and her parents watching some show on Netflix I had never even heard of.

"Hi, honey! How was your day?" she asks me.

"It was okay, I guess," I shrug.

"Do you want to watch this show with us? It's all about our beautiful earth," my mom offers.

"Oh, no, that's ok. I think I'll just go and lay down before I have to pick up Carly in a couple of hours," I explain.

"Okay, have a good nap, honey!" my mom says before putting the TV back on. I hike upstairs, chuckling at my mom. I'll always be her little boy. I walk into my room, where I take off my leather jacket and put it over my chair. I don't actually want to lay down, but it was better than watching whatever my family was watching. I put my air pods in my ears and play some music while I lay on my bed and put my hat over my face. I manage to drift off to sleep after playing "Born To Run."

I wake up to my ringer going off. I pop up and grab my phone under my pillow.

"Hello?" I mumble through the phone.

"Tyler? Where are you? I'm standing outside and it's cold," Carly complains. I look at the time. I was supposed to be there ten minutes ago.

"Crap, I didn't think I was actually going to fall asleep. I'll be there soon," I quickly hang up the phone and get changed. I never know what to wear to fancy restaurants, so usually I just throw on a cotton t-shirt and put a leather jacket over it. I know it's not exactly fancy, but it's the best I can do. I grab the keys off my desk and head downstairs. My family is still watching that documentary.

"I'm leaving," I say to them. My mom's eyes are glued to the TV, and she doesn't even turn around to look at me.

"Okay, have fun," she chimes and waves me off.

I walk outside and get into the car. I drive to Carly's hotel, where in fact, she is standing outside. Carly is wearing a pink dress with a bow tied in the back. I never understood why girls went all out for these kinds of things. When Carly see's my car, she marches over and gets in. She crosses her arms and looks straight ahead. I can tell she's angry.

"I'm sorry for being late," I say as I pull out of the parking lot.

"Whatever, can you just hurry up? I'm hungry," Carly huffs. I nod my head and continue to drive. When we arrive at the restaurant, Carly and I get out of the car.

"Wow, this place is like a palace," Carly says in amazement.

"I know, and they have amazing food, too. C'mon," I say, holding the door for her.

We walk in and a worker asks for my name. As I'm saying my name, I hear Carly gasp. I turn around.

"What's wrong?" I ask her.

"Isn't that Lexi?" Carly asks, a little too loud. Loud enough for Lexi to look directly at me.

"Carly are you crazy?" I whisper to her.

"Sorry," she whispers back. I glance over at Lexi's table again. She's with Carl and Amelia, and of course James, who has his arm around her. After Lexi says something to her table, Carl turns his head.

"Tyler! Come over here, man!" Carl says. I look at Carly and gulp. I seriously want to die right now. I walk over to their table with Carly right next to me. Lexi eyes Carly, then looks at me.

"So you two are together?" Lexi questions us, then looks at James, "not that I would care or anything."

"We are not together," Carly answers her question.

"Wanna join us?" Carl offers.

"Carl!" Amelia scowls.

"Uh, sure," I say.

I don't really want to join them, but at least I can keep an eye on James and Lexi.

Carl and Amelia make just enough room for Carly to sit down. I look over at James and wait for him to move over. After we stare at each other long enough for things to get awkward, he finally moves over, allowing me to sit next to Lexi.

"So, how did you two meet?" James asks me and Carly. I give Carly a look telling her that I'm not going to answer.

"Well, Tyler and the guys were throwing the football around and they caught me staring at Tyler. So, after the boys talked Tyler into it, he finally came over to talk to me,"

Carly explains. I can't keep my eyes off of Lexi. I try to fight the urge, but she's just so damn beautiful. She takes a quick glance at me before continuing on with the conversation.

"I will never forget the day I met James. He got lost and didn't know where he was going. Luckily, he found me, and I was heading in the same direction. I am so happy we met," Lexi says, grabbing James' hand.

"You are just so cute," James says to her.

"I love you," she says to him. I want to throw up. Seriously, I don't feel good.

Carly looks at me and gives me a warm smile. Thank god she's here. I don't know what I would do without her.

CHAPTER 23

LEXI

Ok fine, I was trying to make Tyler jealous. But he deserves it! I just want to show him what he missed.

"So, Lexi, I hear you want to go to Harvard," Carly tells me. I roll my eyes. Seriously, Tyler? You talk to Carly about me?

"Um, well that's where my mom wants me to go," I say.

"Lexi is so smart. She can get into any college she wants to," James announces.

"Yeah, I know," Tyler says. I give him a quick look before focusing my attention back on James.

"James is an amazing swimmer. And he is so strong, and handsome, don't ya think?" I say, smiling. He kisses my forehead.

"I think that I would rather be anywhere but here," I hear Tyler mumble.

"That's great!" Carly says. Man is this girl annoyingly cheerful.

"Well, if you'll excuse me, I have to use the ladies room," I say. I don't really have to go, but I just need some space. I make a quick pit stop to the bar area and order water.

"Here you go," the waiter says, handing it to me.

"Thank you." I take a sip and sit there for a moment to collect my thoughts before I stand up. As I head back to the table, someone grabs my arm and pulls me around the corner.

"What do you think you're doing?" Tyler whispers

"I just ordered water. Am I doing something wrong?" I ask innocently.

"Yes, you won't shut up about how amazing James is, and blah, blah, blah," Tyler says, annoyance evident in his tone.

"Well, I'm sorry that I'm so in love with my boyfriend," I fight back.

"You're trying to make me jealous, aren't you?" he asks me.

"What? No. But if I am, is it working?" I ask him.

"Yes, of course it's working. It should be me that you're talking about, not him," Tyler whispers even louder.

"Yeah, well I gave you another chance when I drove to Connecticut. Only I wasn't the one with you. It was Carly," I whisper back, just as loud.

"Well, excuse me, but you made it very clear that you were done with me. How was I supposed to know that you were coming to Connecticut? Maybe if you actually picked up the phone, then—"

"Is everything okay back here?" a waiter asks us. We both turn our heads at the same time.

"Yes, everything's fine. We were just leaving," I tell him. I give Tyler one last look before walking back to the table.

"Hey babe," James says, putting his arm around me. A few minutes later, Tyler walks up.

"Did you call your mom?" Carly asks.

"Yes, unfortunately we're just not seeing eye to eye right now," Tyler says looking at me.

* * *

"He just drives me crazy!" I yell at my older sister as she watches me pull out my hair. "I am so sick and tired of him always pulling me aside. All we ever do is fight!"

"Calm down. He still likes you. Just give him time," she tells me.

"Give him time? He's had time! He moved to Connecticut, remember?" Just then I hear a knock on the door.

"I got it," I grumble. I open the door.

"Lexi!" Bianca says, hugging me.

"Bianca, hi. I wasn't expecting you."

"I know, I just missed you. So, tell me how everything has been."

"It's fine," I mutter.

"Are you okay?" she asks me.

"I don't want to talk about it," I say to her.

"Well, what do you want to talk about?" she asks me.

"Nothing, Bianca," I snap.

She steps back and looks at me. "What has gotten into you?"

"I just really want to be left alone. My life has been crazy, and I don't want to talk about it, especially with you, miss gossip queen," I call her. Her eyes go wide.

"Is that really what you think of me?" she asks me. I shrug.

"It's what everyone thinks of you," I say nonchalantly.

"You know what, Lexi, screw you. You have everything you have ever wanted.

You have two boys who are practically on their knees begging you to love them. You are the smartest person I know who can get into any college you want to. It's always about you. When was the last time you asked me about my life, huh? I have been there through everything. I'm the one that helped you through the breakup. Not Tyler, not James, me. But I get it. Your life is so hard that you can't talk about it with your own best friend."

"What? No, Bianca—"

She puts her hand up. "Save it for Tyler." She walks away. I storm to my room and slam the door shut. Tears come streaming down my face as I think about everything I've done. I have been a terrible friend to Bianca and I hadn't even realized it. I didn't tell James that Tyler kissed me, even though I should have. And to top it off, I practically hate my family. How could I have been so stupid? My life just got so messed up, and it's all my fault.

CHAPTER 24

TYLER

"Lexi still likes you," Carly says to me. I look at her.

"How do you know?" I ask her.

"I saw the way she looked at you. She's only with James to make you jealous."

"Carly, we're leaving in a couple of days to go back to Connecticut. She'll forget about me and still be with James. I really screwed up big time," I say.

"Tyler, can I be frank?" she asks me. I nod my head. "I know right now it might seem like the end of the world, but there are many other girls out there. You'll date other girls until you find the one. Eventually, you and Lexi will grow up, move apart from each other, and only see one another at the high school reunions," Carly tells me. I blink. Her saying those words feels like I've just been shot in the stomach.

"That's not true. Lexi and I are soulmates," I say.

She shakes her head. "That's what they all say. My boyfriend, Tom, and I did everything together, just like you and Lexi. Since I moved to Connecticut, do you know how many times I've talked to him?"

"No," I reply.

"Once, and that was because I left my sweatshirt at his place and he didn't know my new address," she tells me.

"Okay, but Lexi and I are different," I fight her.

"Oh my god, Tyler," she throws her hands up, "You two are not different. You're 18, she's 17. You guys have your whole life ahead of you. You can't pine after her forever."

In the back of my mind I know Carly's right, but I don't want her to be. I know a married couple who were high school sweethearts. We can be like that, too. I don't want to be with anyone else but her. I love Lexi. She's beautiful, kind, funny, and warmhearted. She's perfect, and I never want to lose her

CHAPTER 25

LEXI

I pace back and forth in my room. Tears are flowing down my face as I think of a way to fix this, but nothing comes to mind. Everything in my life is screwed up. What do I do? Everyone hates me: Bianca, my mom, even Tyler, who I always thought would be there for me. How could things get so out of hand? When I was a little girl, I always knew what I wanted. Instead of playing with dolls, I would read books. Instead of coloring in a coloring book, I would write stories. There was only one path for me, and that was Harvard. Mainly because ever since I was four, that was all my mother would talk about with me. That's all I knew. Now my whole world is falling apart, and I don't know how to stop it. I grab my coat and keys, not knowing where exactly I'm going.

"Where are you going?" Amelia asks me as I open the door.

"Out. I need to think," I tell her.

"No, don't. It's dark and snowing out," Amelia warns me. I look at her through my watery eyes, then walk out the door.

As I'm driving around, I look at the little children playing in the snow. I give a little smile. I never had fun like that. I never built a snowman or made a snow angel, and it was all because of my mother. How could she do that to me? How can she rob me of my childhood? The more I think about it, the angrier I get. The tears keep flowing from my eyes as I hit the steering wheel three times, trying to get my anger out. As I look back at the road I notice headlights coming right at me.

What the—

BOOM.

CHAPTER 26

TYLER

My mom, Carly, and I are sitting at the family table playing monopoly. Every time we have guests over, my mom always insists we play.

"I think I'll buy this property," Carly says, handing my mom $150 in monopoly dollars.

"Tyler, your turn," my mom says. Just as I'm about to roll the dice, my phone vibrates on the table.

"Hold on," I say to my mom and Carly. I grab my phone and stand up.

"What's up, Bianca?" I answer.

"Tyler," Bianca sobs.

"What's wrong?" I ask her. When she doesn't answer I ask again. "Bianca, tell me what happened," I demand.

"It's Lexi. She's been in an accident."

My eyes go wide and I feel like the world just stopped. All I can think about is getting to Lexi. I run to the door and grab my keys and coat.

"Where are you going?" my mom asks. I don't answer as I open the door and run outside. I call Bianca from the car and find out where Lexi is. I arrive at the hospital and spot Lexi's family and Bianca in the waiting room.

"Where is she?" I ask her mom.

"Tyler—"

"Look, I get it. You don't like me. But I'm in love with your daughter. So please, tell me where she is," I beg.

"No, Tyler, I wasn't going to tell you that you couldn't see her. I was going to tell you that we haven't been allowed to see her yet. The doctor hasn't said anything yet,"

"Oh," I say. I sit in a chair and wait. And wait. And wait.

"It's all my fault," I hear Bianca whisper next to me. I look at her.

"What are you talking about?" I ask. She looks at me and wipes a tear from her cheek.

"We had a huge fight right before she got in the car accident. It's all my fault," she repeats herself.

"Don't blame yourself, Bianca, it's no one's fault. These things happen," I reassure her. Finally, a doctor comes out. I stand up just as the doctor makes his way over to her parents.

"You can see her now. She isn't awake yet, but she's stable," the doctor tells us. Her parents and Amelia go in first. I look at Bianca, who has her head in her lap. I sit back down next to her and squeeze her hand. She looks at me and gives me a small smile before crying again.

After waiting for about 30 minutes, her family walks back into the living room. I can tell that Amelia was crying. A lot.

"You can see her now," Amelia says, on the verge of crying again. I nod my head.

"Do you wanna come?" I ask Bianca.

"No, you go ahead. I'm not ready to see her yet," she replies. I squeeze her hand before getting up and walking to the room. I slowly open the door and look at her. As soon as I see her it's like I can't breathe anymore. She has cuts all over her face and hands. I was told that she got a huge piece of glass stuck in her leg that they removed, and she had to get several stitches for the wound. The doctor said that she hit her head so hard on the airbag that it knocked her out right away and she's been unconscious ever since. I can't believe this happened to Lexi. I walk over to her and touch her hand. She's such a good person. She doesn't deserve this.

★ ★ ★

I wake up to the sound of my name being called. "Tyler, she's awake," Amelia informs me. I pop right up.

"You're kidding," I say to her.

"Nope, come and see for yourself," she says.

I walk into the room where her parents and Bianca are hovering over her.

"Lexi?" I say.

"Hi, Tyler," Lexi mumbles. She's still pretty out of it. Her eyes are half closed and she sounds so weak when she talks.

"Thank god you're okay," I say, my voice shaking. We hear a

knock on the door and a nurse walks in.

"I heard my favorite patient's awake," she smiles, clipboard in one hand.

"You say that to everyone," Lexi breathes out. I chuckle under my breath. Even in a hospital, Lexi still manages to crack jokes. How can anyone hate her?

"But this time I mean it. Anyways, now that you're awake, we would like to run a few tests on you. Your family and friends can wait outside. This might take a while," the nurse says to us.

"Okay, we'll be in the waiting room. I love you, honey," her dad says with a smile rubbing her cheek.

"I love you, too," she smiles. We all make our way to the waiting room, where we sit for the next four hours.

CHAPTER 27

LEXI

Finally I'm done with all the tests. I'm still in a lot of pain, especially my leg. The doctor helped me prop my leg up on a pillow to ease the pain. Apparently I lost a lot of blood. As I'm flicking through the channels on the tv in my small room, I hear the door open and close.

"Lexi?"

"Hey, Tyler." I give him a small smile.

"Need some company?" he asks me. After thinking about it, I make room for him on my bed. He smiles and comes to sit next to me.

"Your family and Bianca went to get some food. They asked if you want anything," he tells me.

"No, I'm okay, I don't really have much of an appetite right now," I inform him. He grabs my hand and holds it.

"Wanna tell me what happened?"

"No, not really," I say. The last thing I need is for Tyler to know that my whole life is falling apart. He will just run away again, and I don't really want him to leave just yet.

"Okay, whatever you say, boss. What are we watching?" he asks.

* * *

I spent the rest of the afternoon talking to Tyler. I haven't laughed this much since he left, and it felt good to be with him. As much as I like James, he doesn't make me feel the way that I feel with Tyler. We haven't been able to talk like this in a long time. It's almost like we're talking as … friends. Would that be such a bad thing? To be just friends with Tyler? I mean, it is possible, right? As we're in the middle of watching a movie, someone comes barging into my room, making both me and Tyler jump.

"James?" My eyes go wide.

"Oh my god, baby, what happened?" he says, kissing my lips. Part of me is mad at James for ruining my moment with Tyler, but after all, James is my boyfriend.

"How did you know I was in here?" I ask him.

"Who doesn't know? The whole town's talking about it," James tells me.

"Oh wow, how embarrassing," I laugh.

"Thanks, man, for watching her, but I'm here now. You can leave," James says to Tyler.

"Sorry, man, but I'm not leaving," Tyler says.

"Are you stupid? You're not her boyfriend anymore. I am, so leave," James demands. Tyler stands up and looks James right in the eyes.

"I'm not leaving," Tyler says slowly.

"Guys," I say, trying to calm them down.

"She doesn't want you here. If she was still into you, you would be her boyfriend, but obviously she's over you," James says.

"She still loves me, you're just too oblivious to notice," Tyler fights back.

"Guys," I say again, more sternly.

"You don't want to mess with me, not when it comes to Lexi," James says, stepping closer to Tyler.

"Are you seriously trying to tell me that you love Lexi more than I do? Back off of her unless you want to end up right here in the hospital," Tyler threatens.

"Guys!" I yell. They both look at me. "Both of you out, now."

"What?" James asks.

"You heard me, get out," I repeat again.

"C'mon, Lexi. We were having fun before James got here. Just tell him to leave, and we can finish the movie," Tyler says to me.

"I want to be alone. Please, get out," I demand, crossing my arms.

"This is all your fault," Tyler growls, hitting James with his shoulder as he walks past him.

"My fault?" James asks, following him. Once the door is shut I let out a breath. *What just happened?*

CHAPTER 28

TYLER

I think I screwed up, big time. I know Lexi wants us to get along, but I just want to slap that grin off of James' face. Who does he think he is? He can't just walk in and start barking out orders. I have known Lexi for two years, and he has known her for a couple months. As I'm sitting in the park staring out into the water, I notice a girl skipping up to me. As she gets closer I realize it's Kayla, one of the girls I flirted with before I started dating Lexi.

"Hey, Tyler!" she says, taking a seat next to me.

"What's up?" I ask.

"I heard you were back in town." She smiles.

"You heard correctly."

"You busy tonight? A couple of people are getting together at Brad's house. His parents are going out for like the whole night and he said that there is going to be alcohol there," she says.

"Kayla, do you think I'm a fun guy?" I ask.

"Well, you were fun until you met Lexi. Then you stopped partying and kinda became a loser," Kayla says, making fun of me.

"Well, you can tell Brad that I'll be there," I reply, nodding my head.

Some may say that I'm doing this out of revenge to get back at Lexi. She made me promise that I'd quit drinking so much once I started dating her. I of course agreed because I was so in love with her, but now she's with James. She chose him over me, and there's nothing I can do about it. Why? Because soon I'm going back to Connecticut, while he will still be here. With her.

A couple of days have passed and I'm really not looking forward to going back to Connecticut. I have to leave in two days, and I'm dreading it. I have had so much fun. I went to parties and did things that I haven't done in two years. I didn't realize how much Lexi was holding me back. I feel free. I'm sitting on the top of a table with a girl named Alexandra at the park. She brought a pack of cigarettes and offered me one, which I gladly accepted.

I just met Alexandra a couple of days ago. She goes to another school and her and Kayla are best friends. As we're sitting there, I hear my name being called. I look behind me then groan. *Great, just the person I want to see...* She looks at me in horror when she realizes what I'm doing.

"Lexi, you're out of the hospital," I say in a very steady voice as I exhale a puff of

smoke.

"Yeah, they released me yesterday. What's going on?"

"Nothing, Lexi, you're not my girlfriend, and you can't control my actions anymore. How did you know I was even here?" I ask her.

"I stopped by your house and your grandmother told me you

were here. Are you actually smoking?" she asks me.

"Maybe I should go. Are you still coming to that party tonight?" Alexandra asks me.

"What party?" Lexi asks.

"There's a party at Jace's house tonight," Alexandra answers.

"Well then, I'll be there," Lexi says, puffing out her chest like she's proud.

"Great, see you tonight." Alexandra adds, before walking away. I hop off the table and look at her

"Are you out of your mind? You are not going to a party tonight," I say to her.

"You're not my boyfriend, Tyler," Lexi mocks me.

"Oh my god, stop being so difficult. You just got out of the hospital. You should be resting. Besides, it's at Jace's house. That guy is clearly a creep," I say to her, remembering what happened the last time Lexi went to a party at his house.

"I'm going, and there's nothing you can say or do to stop me," she says walking away.

Man this girl is stubborn

CHAPTER 29

LEXI

I hurt Tyler, and he's taking it out on me. He's trying to make me feel the same pain he felt, and it's working. I get ready for this stupid party that I don't even want to go to. I still feel pretty weak from the car accident. My leg is all taped up and so are my ribs. Thank god it's winter so no one will ask questions. I call Bianca and ask her to give me a ride because I'm too scared to drive. After waiting for about ten minutes, she texts me that she's here. I grab my phone and run out of the house.

"Hey," Bianca says.

"Hey," I say back.

"How are you?" she asks me.

"I'm doing better," I reply.

"Well, that's good." After a moment of silence she starts speaking again. "So listen, I owe you an apology. I never should've freaked out on you like that. You were stressed and I should've realized that."

"No, I owe you an apology. I have been making everything about me. You mean so much to me and I really don't want our friendship to end. I love you so much and I honestly couldn't imagine my life without you," I tell her. She smiles.

"Okay, enough sappy talk. Let's have some fun!" Bianca says, making me laugh.

We arrive at Jace's house and walk inside. I feel uneasy being in the same house that made me feel so worthless, but I still care for Tyler and I'll do anything to make sure he stays out of trouble. He's clearly not thinking straight at the moment. I head to the kitchen in hopes of finding Tyler, but he's nowhere to be found.

"C'mon Lexi, stop worrying about him. Have fun," Bianca says, hip bumping me.

"Yeah, I know, but what if he does something stupid?" I ask her. Bianca starts dancing around me.

"Who cares? Dance!" she encourages.

I laugh and turn my head, only to spot Tyler in the corner. He's with a group of friends, laughing, taking sips out of a red solo cup. Great, he's drunk.

"Wait, I found him," I yell over the loud music. I march over there and tap on his shoulder.

"Someone's in trouble," the guys mumble.

Five months ago, I never would have done this, but after everything that's happened since then, confronting Tyler in front of his friends is nothing.

"Just go away, Lexi. Can't you see I'm having fun?" he says to me. Yup, definitely drunk. His breath reeks of alcohol.

"Why are you being like this?" I ask him.

"Like what? I'm just being me," he slurs. The guys chuckle as they listen to every word we say.

"No, you're not. This isn't you. The Tyler I know would never do this. Please, can I just take you home," I beg him.

"Then I guess you don't really know me as well as you thought you did," he fights back.

"Tyler, please," I say

"No, you do not get to tell me to do anything. I have been nothing but kind and compassionate to you, and all you ever did was treat me like garbage. So guess what, Lexi? I'm done. I'm done chasing you all around when you're clearly not interested in me anymore. So just go back to your boyfriend and just leave me alone," he slurs.

"Tyler—"

"Go away," he demands, turning his back on me. I'm on the verge of tears, but I can't let anyone see me cry. As I walk away, I feel my arm being pulled into a separate hallway.

"What the hell!"

"Aw, did your boyfriend reject you?" Jace pouts.

"He's not my boyfriend." I cross my arms.

"You are a worthless piece of shit, you know that?" Jace says.

"Excuse me?" I raise my eyebrows.

"You are such a little bitch. Tyler completely embarrassed me at my own school.

It was humiliating, and it was all because of you. You can't keep your damn mouth shut for more than two minutes without running to Tyler," he rambles, beginning to raise his voice. I hate confrontation, and right now I feel like a lost puppy in the middle of the woods.

"Jace, not now," I say.

"Everyone thinks you're this big shot Harvard girl, but you're just a big phony. I see right through your little act."

"I don't have to sit here and listen to this," I say as I try to walk past him, but he blocks me.

"Oh, but you do. See, Tyler got everything. He got quarterback, he got the popularity, he got the girl, and he doesn't deserve any of it. Don't you get it, Lexi? He doesn't care about you. Never has, never will."

"Think again, asshole," Tyler says from behind Jace. He grabs Jace by the shirt and throws him against the wall. He takes Jace's wrists in one hand and punches him in the stomach.

"You really are testing my patience, aren't you?" Tyler says, punching Jace in the stomach again. Jace lets out a grunt as Tyler continues to punch him. For once, I don't stop Tyler. Jace has hurt me and it's time to knock some sense into him.

"If you ever even say a word to her again, I will not hesitate to kill you," Tyler says, letting go of his wrists. Jace takes a look at me, then stalks away. Tyler grabs me by the arm and pulls me into a hug.

"I'm so sorry," he says, starting to cry. I've never seen Tyler cry before. It's probably because he's still drunk and can't handle all of these emotions.

"It's not your fault," I reassure him.

"Yes, it is. I shut you out. You wouldn't even be here if it wasn't for me," he continues to sob on my shoulder.

"Tyler, seriously, I'm fine. Please don't blame yourself."

***

Bianca drives me and Tyler to his grandparents' house. Even though he hadn't had a drink in an hour, he still wasn't sober enough to drive. I insisted on staying with him. Tyler is sort of a mess right now, and honestly, I want to be with him. We go up to his room where he takes off his shirt and throws it to the ground. I try to look away, but my eyes can't help but stare. I haven't seen his rock hard abs since we broke up, and it's hard to resist admiring them.

"I'm sorry again for what happened," he says to me.

I throw my hands in the air. "For the hundredth time, stop apologizing!"

"You know you can come in, right?" he says to me. I look down and realize I'm still standing outside of his room. I nod my head and take a few steps inside.

"Are you okay?" I ask, concerned. Tyler has been acting out and I'm actually worried about him. He hasn't been this way in years, and I don't know what he's capable of.

"I'm okay. I was just upset and needed to let loose. But you're right, this isn't me, and this isn't who I want to be," he says to me.

"Can I ask you a question?" I ask him.

"Sure, anything," he answers.

"Why did you fall in love with me? I mean, I watched you at the party and with those girls, and it looked like you were having fun. Why date me when you could be the most popular guy with all the girls you want?" I ask him. He looks at me.

"Honestly?" he asks.

"Honestly."

"Because you're the most beautiful girl I have ever seen. You are kind, gentle, and the hardest working person I know. You have this drive in you that is hard to find in other girls, and something drew me to you that I just couldn't resist. I know there are others girls out there, but none of them are you." He takes a step towards me. "Tell me you don't have any feelings for me. Tell me that right now and I'll back away. I'll go back to Connecticut and you'll never hear another word from me again. But if you don't, well you know what I'll do." His face comes closer to me and I gulp. He licks his lips.

"Go on, tell me," he whispers as he looks me straight in the eyes. I feel my knees wobble as his hand slightly brushes my arms.

"I, um, I can't tell you that," I say, having to grip onto his desk so I don't fall over.

He uses his pointer finger to lift my chin up.

"I love you so much," before planting a long kiss on me.

* * *

I wake up to the sound of birds chirping and the sun shining. I have a big smile on my face as I make my way down the stairs and grab an apple.

"Morning, Amelia," I smile as I take a bite out of my apple.

"Well, someone's in a good mood."

"Today just feels…different. I'll catch ya later," I say, before making my way upstairs.

At around noon there's a knock on the door. Who would be here on a Sunday? I don't think my sister invited anyone over. I walk to the door and open it, then my smile fades. Oh god, I forgot I had a boyfriend.

"James? What are you doing here?" I ask.

"Lexi, I am so sorry for my behavior at the hospital. I know you want us to get along, and how I acted was unacceptable. If you want the two of us to be friends, then I'll do my best to make it work," he says to me.

"No, it's okay, don't worry about it," I tell him. My guilty conscience is taking over as I realize I just cheated on him. I don't even know what to say to him.

"So, are we good?" he asks me.

"So good," I say, not really meaning it. He gives me a quick kiss on the lips then hugs me.

"So are you busy right now?" he asks.

"No, what do you want to do?"

"Let's go to Tyler's house. You want us to get along, right? Well the first step is for me to apologize to him," he tells me. My eyes go wide.

"No, James, I don't think that's a good idea."

"You're right, it's not a good idea. It's a great idea. Let's go," he says grabbing my hand.

"Seriously, you don't have to do this," I say as he drags me along the grass.

"Lexi, just get in the car," he demands. I sigh but give in. There's no point in arguing. James doesn't know what I did, and I plan on keeping it that way. I can't act any more suspicious than I already am.

CHAPTER 30

TYLER

"And she just let you kiss her?" Carly asks me.

"Yup, she didn't push away or anything. It was amazing," I tell her.

"Aw, I'm happy for you. Truly," Carly says. The doorbell rings.

"I'll be right back," I walk downstairs and open the door. I look at James, then at Lexi. What is going on? Did she tell him about last night?

"Hey, man, we need to talk," James says. Oh my god, she did tell him.

"I am so sorry James," I blurt out.

James looks at me in shock. "I came over here to apologize to you," James says.

"Why would you apologize to me? It's all my fault, don't blame Lexi," I tell him.

"Why would I blame Lexi? She didn't do anything wrong," James says.

"It just kind of happened," I say. James looks at Lexi, then back to me.

"Are we talking about the same thing?" James asks me.

"Wait, what are you talking about?" I ask.

"I was talking about our fight at the hospital. Did something happen that I don't know about?" he asks.

Oh no, we weren't talking about the same thing. James looks at Lexi, who has her head down.

"Say something, Lexi," James says in an angry tone.

"Hey, calm down, alright? No need to get mad at Lexi," I defend her.

"Don't tell me what to do idiot. What is going on?"

"Leave her alone," I say, trying to defuse the situation.

"Shut it, Tyler. What happened, Lexi?" James raises his voice.

"We kissed, alright?" Lexi blurts out.

James turns his attention back to me. "You kissed Lexi?" he asks.

"Look, James—"

I can't even finish my sentence before he grabs my shirt and throws me onto the frozen ground outside.

"James!" Lexi exclaims.

"You son of a bitch," James says before punching me in the face, making my nose bleed.

"James, please stop!" Lexi begs.

"She's my girlfriend. How dare you?" James says before punching me in the face again. He's about to punch me again when Lexi grabs his arm.

"James, please," Lexi says. He gets off of me and looks at both of us.

"You two deserve each other," James spits.

"What do you mean?" Lexi asks him.

"What I mean is you've been playing me this whole time. It was always Tyler, right from the start. You played me like a fool. I'm done," he yells at her. I can see tears forming in her eyes.

"No, James, please," she cries.

"Just leave me alone!" he gets in his car and drives away. Lexi breaks down in tears as I struggle to stand up. She looks at me and wipes away her tears.

"Here, let me help," she says, grabbing my arm to help me keep balance.

"Lexi, I am so sorry," I tell her.

"It's not your fault. This whole mess is because of me. I should've been honest right from the beginning," she says putting her head down.

"Don't blame yourself," I try to calm her down.

"Tyler?" Carly says from my porch. I look at her and she gasps.

"Oh my god, what happened?" she says running towards us.

"Lexi's boyfriend happened," I tell her.

"Ex-boyfriend," Lexi corrects me. I know this might sound wrong, but hearing Lexi say ex-boyfriend makes me feel amazing inside.

"Aw, Lexi, I'm so sorry," Carly says, giving her a hug.

"I'm fine," Lexi sniffs.

"Yeah, I'm okay, too, thanks for checking up on me Carly," I say sarcastically.

"Wow someone's in a mood," Carly says.

"Well, I'm sorry, but I did just get punched in the face," I point out.

"Okay, Mr. Cranky Pants, how about we get you cleaned up then go out and get something to eat?" Carly suggests.

"I'm down," I reply.

"That sounds great. Oh, and Carly, I just wanted to apologize for being so rude to you before. You really are a good person, and I can understand why you and Tyler are friends," Lexi says to her. Carly smiles.

"Thanks so much, Lexi. I bet we can become friends, too," Carly says, giving Lexi another hug.

"Okay, you two, I have blood running down my nose, so can we get this show on the road?" I ask. Carly and Lexi laugh.

"Hold on," Carly says, running back inside. She returns with some damp paper towels for my nose. After cleaning myself up the best that I can, Carly says, "Let's go."

We arrive at the small ice cream shop in the center of town, where Lexi and I used to go all the time when we were dating. We would sit in the pink booth in the corner and feed each other ice cream. The three of us walk up to the counter, where a girl in her mid-twenties greets us.

"How may I help you?" the kind woman asks.

"I'll have strawberry ice cream, please," Carly says.

"And for you, sir?" she asks me.

"I'll have the butter pecan ice cream, and this girl will have chocolate ice cream with hot fudge and sprinkles," I answer for Lexi.

"Sure, coming right up," she says before scooping up some strawberry ice cream.

"You remembered my order." Lexi smiles.

"Of course I do. I remember everything about you," I reply. She returns with our ice cream and I hand her $15.

"Have a good day," she says, smiling, before going into the storage area.

"Let's sit there," I say, looking at the corner booth. Lexi looks at me and gives me a small smile. Looks like she remembers our special spot as well. I sit next to Lexi as Carly sits in front of us.

"I'm glad that we can do this. I was worried that you were never doing to like me,"

Carly says to Lexi.

"I guess I just got a little jealous of you," Lexi admits with a small shrug. I look at her.

"And why would you be jealous?" I smile.

"Oh, shut up," she says, trying to hide a smirk

CHAPTER 31

LEXI

I actually had a great time with Carly and Tyler. I was a little worried because I didn't know where Carly and Tyler stood as far as a relationship goes, but it seems like they are just friends, which is a huge relief.

"Thanks for a great time. I really needed it after the whole James fiasco," I say as we arrive back at Tyler's grandparents' house.

"No problem, it was fun," Carly replies.

"Well, I better get going. My mom is probably wondering where I am," I tell them.

"Do you need a ride?" Carly asks.

"No, it's alright, I think I'd rather just walk."

I don't want to admit this to Carly and Tyler, but I need time to think. I do feel terrible about what I did to James. I guess he was right. I didn't realize at the time, but I was only using him to get to Tyler. What kind of person does that? I never thought in a million years that I would cheat on someone. I always looked down on those type of people, and yet I, myself, cheated. James loved me and was kind. He deserved better.

"I'll come with you," Tyler says.

"I'm okay with going alone. It's only a few blocks away."

"I know, but I want to go," Tyler replies. I smile at his comment.

"Well then let's go."

As we're walking back, he grabs my hand, making me tingle. Call me crazy, but it feels right. It's like my hand belongs in his.

"You're cute when you're nervous," Tyler smirks. *My face turns red. He knows I'm nervous. How embarrassing.*

"I don't know what you're talking about." I shrug, hoping I convinced him that I'm not anxious.

"So, listen, I wanted to say that I'm sorry about James," Tyler says to me.

"No, Tyler, I'm not mad at you," I tell him.

"Let me finish. I said I want to, but the truth is, I'm not sorry," he stops me and makes me look him straight in the eyes.

"Lexi, I'm in love with you and I'm not afraid to admit it. I need you to be with me.

Don't you get that? I physically need to hold you in my arms. I can't be in this crazy world without you by my side," he says. I shake my head.

"It can't work. You're in Connecticut and I'm in Massachusetts. Long distance relationships never work. I'll never see you. How can we build a strong relationship if we never see each other?" I ask.

"We already built a strong relationship. We have spent every day together for the last two years," he comments.

"Tyler, no, okay? Please just try to understand from my point of view," I beg.

"Fine, come with me to Connecticut for the week," he says.

I laugh, thinking it's a joke, but when I look at him in the eyes, I can tell that he's serious.

"Are you insane? I have school this week."

"C'mon, Lexi, be a little adventurous. Just ask your mom. You never know until you ask," he begs.

"Tyler," I sigh.

"Lexi, just ask," he says to me. He grabs my arm and looks at me with his cute brown eyes. "Please." There's no way I can say no when he's touching me.

"Fine, I'll ask, but there's no promises. Don't get your hopes up," I say to him.

***

"Mom, I'm home!" I say, walking through the door. She walks in the living room holding a towel to dry her hands.

"Hi, Alexa, how was your day?" she asks me.

"It was okay," I shrug.

"Okay, well I hope you're hungry. I'm making spaghetti," she says, walking away.

"Oh, wait!" I say to her. She turns and faces my direction.

"Yes?"

I take a deep breath. *Here goes nothing.*

"I have a question to ask. It's kind of a big one, so I totally get it if you say no.

Tyler asked me to go to Connecticut with him. It would only be for this week," I say, sucking in my breath.

"You want to go to Connecticut?" she asks me. I nod my head. After a long pause she finally answers.

"You can go."

I sigh. "I unders—wait, what?"

"Alexa, you had a really traumatizing experience. You need a break. As long as Tyler's mom will be with you and him at all times, you can go," she says to me.

"Oh my god! Thank you so much!" I say giving her the biggest hug.

"I mean it, Alexa, you can't be goofing off every minute of every day. I want you to email all your teachers and ask for your work so you aren't behind when you return."

"I will. Thank you again!"

CHAPTER 32

TYLER

It feels so surreal that Lexi is actually here with me. I thought for sure that her mom was going to say no.

"I cannot believe you're actually here right now," I say to her.

"I can't believe I'm here, either," she answers. We pull into our driveway and my mom turns to face us in the backseat.

"Now listen. I know that you came here to spend time with each other, and I am more than happy to have you with us," my mom says, looking at Lexi, "but I do have a few rules."

"Absolutely," Lexi says, nodding along.

"Lexi we have a guest room that you can sleep in. I am sorry, but you two cannot sleep in the same room. I promise I will not get in your way if you both follow the rules.

Do we have an agreement?" she asks.

"Yes, I promise, I won't be a problem," Lexi says. My mom looks at me.

"Tyler?" she asks, waiting for a response.

"Yup," I groan. I really wanted to sleep in the same room as Lexi. I don't want to leave her side for this entire week.

"Good." She turns back around.

Lexi looks at me, and she knows exactly what I'm thinking. She lays her head on my shoulder and shuts her eyes. Man, she's gorgeous. I love this girl so much that I don't know how I'm ever going to let her leave at the end of this week. We get out of the car and I grab Lexi's suitcase.

"Thanks, Tyler," she says, smiling.

I nod my head and bring her to our guest room. I lay her suitcase across the bed and she looks around.

"Your house is really nice," Lexi says.

"Yeah? I liked my house better in Massachusetts," I say. She nods her head and sits on the bed.

"I'm happy that you're here," I say, leaning against the wall.

"I am, too. Life without you has not been the same." She tucks her hair behind her ear and sighs.

"No one has been giving you a hard time, have they?" I ask, narrowing my eyes at her.

"No. I mean, every time I walk past Jace and his friends they always whisper and laugh, but I don't care. It doesn't really bother me," She shrugs. I sit next to her and look right into her eyes.

"I'm so sorry, Lexi. I should be there." I grab her hand.

"Wanna show me your room?" she asks me. I laugh. Lexi always knows how to keep my emotions in check.

"Sure." We stand up, still holding hands, and I take her to my room.

"Oh my god," she says, walking over to my desk. I laugh. I knew she was gonna love that picture. She picks it up and looks at me.

"I can't believe you still have it." She smiles.

"Lexi, it was a gift from you, I would never throw it out," I say. For my seventeenth birthday, Lexi drew me a picture of the two of us holding hands. She's actually a pretty decent artist.

"Why?" she asks me.

"Like I said, it was a gift from you," I say. My phone rings. I take it out of my pocket and answer it.

"Sup, Ben," I say.

"I'm having a small get together tonight. You in?" he asks me. I look at Lexi.

"Hold on a sec." I take the phone off my ear. "You cool if we go out tonight? You could meet all my friends," I say. I can tell she's hesitant by the way she bites her lip. "I promise you'll like them," I assure her.

"Ok, we can go."

I smile and put the phone back up to my ear. "I'll be there," I answer.

"Cool, see you tonight." He hangs up, and I slip my phone back in my pocket.

"You are amazing," I say to her.

"Aw stop, you're making me blush," she jokes. I take a step closer to her.

"No seriously, you amaze me," I say, brushing her arm.

"Well, you amaze me, too."

"Don't freak out, but I'm going to kiss you now," I say to her.

Before she can say anything, I grab her face and gently let my lips linger over hers. I have been dreaming of this moment since the day I left. She is finally letting me back in.

"Tyler," my mom walks in. I quickly pull my head away from Lexi's and watch as her face instantly turns red and she practically hides behind me.

"What's up, mom," I say to her. I can tell that my mom feels uncomfortable, but she's trying to act like she didn't see anything.

"Here's your laundry, please put it away," my mom says, handing me a basket full of clothes.

"Will do." I smile. She nods her head and shuts my door, which is probably what I should've done before I kissed Lexi. I look at her, and we start laughing.

"Well, that was a first," Lexi jokes.

"Not for me it wasn't," I say. As soon as the words leave my mouth I realize I've made a mistake.

"What do you mean?" Lexi asks.

"Nothing, it's stupid. Just one time, in freshman year, my mom walked in on me with another girl. But that was before I met you," I say.

"Tyler, I'm not mad. I knew who you were before I started dating you. All the stuff you did before, that's in the past. You don't have to justify yourself," she says.

How could you not love this girl?

CHAPTER 33

LEXI

I finish putting on mascara for this party we are going to.

"You ready?" Tyler yells.

"Almost!" He appears from around the corner.

"You don't need makeup to look pretty," Tyler says.

"That is very sweet." I smile. He walks over to me and puts his arms around me.

We both look in the mirror.

"We look good together," Tyler says.

"Yes, we do," I answer. He kisses my cheek.

"Let's go," he grabs my hand and walks me outside to the car.

He pulls out of the driveway, placing his hand on my thigh and giving it a light squeeze.

"Are your friends nice?" I ask him.

"They are much better than the ones I had back in Massachusetts," he reassures me. He pulls up to Ben's house.

"I love you," Tyler says. I look at him and a smile grows on my face.

"I love you, too," I say. He leans over to kiss me. We get out of the car and go to knock on Ben's door.

"It's open!" I hear a boy yells. Tyler looks at me and grabs my hand, then we walk inside. All of his friends, who are sitting on the couch, look over, and then their mouths drop.

"No way," one of the boys says.

"I can't believe this," another girl whispers. I look at Tyler.

"Lexi!" Carly says, getting up to give me a hug.

"So this is the infamous Lexi. We've heard a lot about you," one boy says as he stands up.

"Lexi, this is Ben. And this is Danny, Andrew, Sabrina, and Nicole," Tyler introduces us. I smile and wave.

"Welcome, come, sit," Andrew says. I sit on the couch and Tyler does the same.

"I'm so glad you're here," Carly says.

"So am I," I say.

I ended up having a great time with Tyler's friends. Sabrina didn't really talk much, but everyone was super nice and asked me a lot of questions. As the night winds down, Tyler puts his arm around me and kisses my cheek. Andrew looks at us.

"You really did a number on our boy," Andrew jokes. I look at Tyler who grins.

"Yeah, and we were here to pick up the pieces," Sabrina says in a serious tone.

Wait, is she for real.

"Well, I'm sorry," I say.

"You should be," Sabrina scoffs. I sit up and wiggle Tyler's arm off of me.

"Do you have a problem with me?" I ask.

"Oh, honey, I have a big problem with you," Sabrina says, leaning forward.

"Sabrina, knock it off," Tyler warns.

She completely ignores him as she looks at me. "Who do you think you are? You break Tyler's heart and then just come walking in here like you own the place? All of these people might be acting nice, but we are all thinking the same thing," Sabrina points out.

"Sabrina!" Carly gasps.

"You don't know me," I say.

"I don't? I don't know that your mom is forcing you to go to Harvard? I don't know that Tyler was not only your first boyfriend, but your first kiss? I don't know that you heated on your new boyfriend and used him? He told us everything about you," Sabrina says.

"Sabrina, stop," Tyler warns her.

"You're such a bitch," I say.

All of a sudden she springs out of her seat and gets in my face, yelling. I can't understand a word she is saying as Tyler quickly wraps his arm around me and brings me to another room. He grabs my wrists to stop me from hitting his chest to let me out.

A tear rolls down my cheek as I grow more and more angry.

"Let me go!" I yell.

"Not until you calm down," Tyler tells me.

"Fine," I say. He releases my wrists and leans back against the door.

"Are you okay?" he asks me.

"Do I look okay? What was her problem?" I ask.

"I don't know, but you're cute when you're angry." Tyler smiles.

"It's not funny!"

"Lexi, it's me," Carly says, lightly knocking on the door.

"You can come in," I say. She opens the door and looks at me.

"Andrew took Sabrina home," Carly informs us.

"What was her deal?" I ask.

"Sabrina has had a crush on Tyler since the day he got here, but he never was interested in her because he wasn't over you. You being here just put the icing on the cake," Carly explains.

"Oh," I say. Tyler's phone lights up.

"My mom just texted. We gotta go," Tyler says. I nod my head.

"Love you," I say to Carly.

"Love you, too." She gives me a hug. "See ya Tyler."

"See ya," he says. I wave one more time before Tyler and I walk out.

We get back to Tyler's house, where we are greeted by his mom.

"Hi guys, did you have fun?" she asks us. I look at Tyler.

"I guess you could say that," he says.

"Well, listen, I need you to go to bed because you have school tomorrow," Mrs. McHale says.

"Wait, you can't be serious. You really expect me to go to school when Lexi's here?" Tyler asks incredulously.

"Actually, I do. Lexi and I will have a great time while you're there. Now go," Mrs. McHale says. Tyler looks at me.

"Fine," he huffs.

"It's okay, Tyler, I have work to do as well. Anyways, I'm pretty tired, too, so I think I'm gonna go to bed," I say.

"Of course, dear. Sleep tight. Tyler will be waking up early, but you sleep in," his mom says.

"Thank you so much for letting me stay here," I say, giving her a hug.

"Anything for you. Goodnight," she says.

I smile and walk into the guest room. Tyler follows and shuts the door behind him. I take my shoes off and sit on the bed.

"You can't sleep in here," I say to him.

"I know, but I wish I could. I'm sorry that my mom is making me go to school," he says with a frown.

"Tyler," I smile, "school is more important. I'm not mad. I actually would've been shocked if she let you miss school."

"But you're more important to me than school," he says.

"Go to bed Tyler. You have to wake up early," I say.

"Can I at least get a kiss goodnight?" he asks. I laugh.

"Just a quick one." I get up and kiss his lips.

"Love you," he says.

"Love you, too," I reply, and he walks out of the room.

I slip into my pajamas and brush my teeth. I crawl in the queen-sized bed, stare up at the ceiling, and sigh. Maybe I shouldn't have broken up with Tyler. I think in the moment I was shocked and hurt that he had been lying to me. We seem to be having so much fun in Connecticut, but what happens when I go back to Massachusetts? Then the fun will stop, and we'll go back to our lives. He might meet a cute girl and fall in love again, and I might meet a cute guy, just like I met James. What am I doing here? All I'm doing is torturing myself. I'm falling head over heels for this guy, but I'm going to have to leave him, and I don't know if I can handle the pain again.

★ ★ ★

"Thank you for these pancakes. They're really good," I say to Tyler's mom.

After my terrible sleep last night, I really needed this. I kept tossing and turning.

All that was on my mind was Tyler.

"You're very welcome." She smiles at me as I take my last bite of pancake and stand up. I take my plate and head to the sink.

"Let me do it," his mom says.

"Oh no, really, I can do it," I say to her.

"Lexi, you are our guest," she points out.

"Yes, but you are letting me stay in your home," I say.

"I have not seen my son this happy since we left Massachusetts. I can't thank you enough for how much you've helped Tyler. He was a troubled boy before he met you," she says, taking the plate from me. I smile.

"Thank you," I say.

"Well listen, I have to get to work. Are you going to be okay by yourself?" she asks me.

"Yes, I'll be fine," I say.

"Alright, I'll see you later tonight," she says, giving me a hug. She walks out of the house.

"Mom, I'm fine," I huff through the phone. She couldn't even give me one day without calling to check up on me.

"You aren't doing anything that could get you in trouble, correct?" she asks me.

I roll my eyes. "No, mother."

"Alexa, don't give me that attitude. I let you go to Connecticut with a boy," she argues.

"You're right, I'm sorry."

Just then Tyler walks inside. He looks at me and smiles, then throws his backpack on the ground.

"Alexa, are you there?" my mom asks me.

"Yes, listen, I gotta go. I'll call you later, I promise." Before she can say another word, I hang up. Tyler sits next to me on the couch.

"How was school?" I ask.

"Terrible. I couldn't stop thinking about you," he says.

"Well, you got any homework?" I ask.

"Yeah, but I'm not gonna do it."

"Tyler, you have to."

"Right, I forgot who I'm talking to," he says. I smile. He knows that I love school.

Some people find that strange, but I like learning new things. It's what keeps me entertained.

"Go, do it," I instruct him.

"Fine," he groans. He gets up, grabs his backpack, and storms upstairs.

CHAPTER 34

TYLER

After what feels like eternity, I finally finish all my homework. I drop my pencil and shake out my hand. I have never written so much in my entire life, mainly because I don't usually do my homework. My teachers are going to be so surprised tomorrow. I walk downstairs and find Lexi watching TV. She looks at me and grabs the remote to pause it.

"That took a while," she says.

"Yeah, well, not everyone is as smart as you," I point out.

"Wanna watch a movie?" she asks.

"Sure, you pick," I say.

"Alright, how about horror?" she asks. I look at her, shocked.

"Since when do you like horror movies?" I ask.

"A lot has changed since you left." She turns her attention back to the tv. Ouch, that one hurt. I guess she's right. I have been gone for a while. It's only normal for a person to change.

"Lexi, I have a question," I say to her.

"What's up?"

"So, my school does this stupid winter back to school dance thing every year for juniors and seniors, and well, I haven't asked anyone yet because I wasn't going to go. But since you're here and the dance is this Friday, I was thinking you and I could go. Together," I say.

She looks at me. "You're asking me to a school dance?" she asks me. I nod my head.

"We don't have to if you don't want to," I quickly say. She smiles.

"I would love to go." A smile grows on my face.

"Okay, great," I say.

"Why were you not going to go?" she asks me.

"Because I couldn't bring myself to ask anyone else. If I did go with a girl, then all I would be thinking about was how much I wanted to be there with you, and that wouldn't be fair," I say. She lays her head on my chest.

"I wish you never moved," she sighs. I kiss her forehead.

"Me too."

CHAPTER 35

LEXI

Tyler's mom pulls into the parking lot at the mall. She's taking me dress shopping for this dance on Friday night since I didn't know I was going to a dance and never packed a dress.

"Honey, I have been trying to get Tyler to a school event for months," his mom laughs.

"Yeah, he hates these kind of things. The only reason why he went to them was because of me," I say, opening the door to the Macy's department store. We make our way to the dress section. I was told that the theme was white, shocker. I grab a bunch of white dresses and head into the changing room while Tyler's mom sits outside. One by one I would walk out in a new dress, but none of them felt right, even though Tyler's mom said I looked beautiful in all of them. As I was walking out holding all the dresses in my hands, a worker approaches us.

"I can take that for you. Did you find everything you need?" she asks while taking the dresses out of my hands.

"Um, actually no. I'm looking for a white dress," I say to her. She looks me up and down.

"I have the perfect dress. What's your size?" she asks me.

"It varies between small and medium," I answer.

"Yup, this dress will do. Follow me," she says. I look at Mrs. McHale, who nods her head. I follow the worker over to a different section in the store. I look at her name tag on her uniform.

"Addison's a pretty name," I say to her. She looks at me and smiles.

"Thank you. My friends call me Addy. You know, I'm not that much older than you. I'm only twenty. Here you go," she says, handing me the dress.

"Oh, where do you go to school?" I ask her.

"I don't go to school. I decided to follow my boyfriend, well ex-boyfriend, to California so he could follow his dreams of being a pro surfer. Well, he got his wish, but I got nowhere. Worst mistake I've ever made. He dumped me on my ass for some surfer chick. I could've been at Florida State right now, but they gave my spot away for this year. Now I'm back in Connecticut, working in my hometown. Sorry, I've said too much. I like to talk a lot. Go, try the dress on!" she says.

I gulp and look at Tyler's mom. Is that what I'm doing? Am I throwing everything away to be with Tyler?

Mrs. McHale rubs my back and whispers, "Go try it on."

She gives me a sincere look and I nod my head. I shuffle back to the dressing room and take my clothes off. I slip the dress on and look in the mirror. It's a short, sparkly, white dress. It's perfect. I walk outside and look at Mrs. McHale. She gasps.

"Oh, Lexi darling, it's perfect!" she gushes.

"Thank you so much, Mrs. McHale." I smile.

"Please, call me Linda. I think we've established a better relationship. I consider you family," she says.

"Well, thank you, Linda. And I consider you my other mom who isn't crazy," I joke.

"Ha! Thank you, Lexi. Now let's buy that dress," she says.

* * *

It's Friday night, which means I have to start getting ready. I'm very nervous to attend this school dance. What if I run into Sabrina again? What if someone spills on my dress? As I finish curling my hair, Tyler walks in.

"I'm excited to see you in that dress," Tyler says. He wraps his arms around me and we look in a mirror. Part of me is happy that I'm with Tyler. He always knows how to make me smile. But I can't get what Addison said out of my mind. Is it true? Am I throwing away all of my dreams to chase Tyler? I shake the thought out of my head. I just want to have fun tonight. I smile at him.

"Now get out so I can get changed," I demand.

"Or I can stay and watch," he jokes.

"Out," I say, pointing towards the door.

"Okay, okay, I'm going."

He walks out, and I grab the dress from the closet and quickly slip it on. I adjust the length and look at myself. I love how it's tight on the top and flows on the bottom. I wonder if Tyler is going to like the open back.

Okay, now I'm ready. I open the door and walk downstairs.

"Oh, Lexi, you look gorgeous," Linda says, appearing from around the corner. I smile and give her a hug.

"Wow," Tyler says from behind me. I turn around and his jaw drops.

"Um, you … you look … um…"

"You look good, too," I say. He smiles and grabs something from off the counter.

"Here you go," he says, handing me a corsage. It's a white flower with a pretty purple bow wrapped around it.

"Well, are you going to put it on me?" I laugh. He nods his head and slips it on my wrist.

"Lexi," Linda says behind me. I turn around and she hands me a flower. I turn back to face Tyler.

"I got something for you, too," I say. He smiles as I pin the flower on his suit.

"Alright, you two, I need a picture," Linda says. Tyler pulls me in and holds me tight as we smile at the camera.

"Let's go," Tyler says, grabbing my hand.

"Bye, Linda," I say.

"Bye, sweetie. Bye, Tyler," she says.

"Bye, mom," Tyler says and we walk out.

I try to calm myself down the whole car ride over. I don't do well in social settings, and I'm just praying that I don't embarrass myself. I guess Tyler saw that I was tense because he puts his hand on my thigh and squeezes it gently, reassuring me that I'm going to be fine.

"How did I get so lucky?" he asks, making me get butterflies in my stomach.

"I could say the same exact thing." I smile. We pull into the parking lot and Tyler quickly gets out of the car to open the door for me.

"Here you go, my lady," he says while holding out his hand.

"Thank you." I step out of the car, and he grabs my hand, taking me inside the banquet hall.

"Lexi!" Carly says while giving me a hug. "You look so pretty!"

"Well, I could say the same about you!" I smile.

"Oh! Let me introduce you to my date. Dan, come here," Carly waves to him. He walks up and stands by her side.

"Dan, this is my friend Lexi. She's from Massachusetts," Carly says.

"Oh, aren't you from there, too?" Dan asks, directing the question to Tyler.

"Yeah," Tyler answers.

"So are you two dating?" I ask.

"Nah, just friends. We've hooked up a couple of times but it didn't really work out," Carly explains.

"You ready to have some fun?" Tyler asks, putting his arm around me.

"Yup, see you around, Carly," I say as we walk past them. We take a seat at a round table and I lay my purse under my chair.

"Wow, this is amazing," I say about the decorations.

"Yup, my school goes all out," he replies.

"Wanna dance?" I suggest.

"Anything for my girl. Let's go," Tyler says, standing up. I follow him to the dance floor where he gently lays his hand on my arm and looks at me straight in the eyes.

"You know I love you, right?" he asks.

"Of course I know that. Why are you saying this?" I ask.

"I just wanted you to know that. Even after you broke up with me, I never stopped," he says.

I lay my head on his chest and he pulls me in for a hug. I never want this moment to end. I wish I never had to leave Tyler, but Addison's words keep creeping in my mind. *No, I'm not going to let it ruin my night.*

"You're so beautiful," Tyler whispers in my ear. All of a sudden he grabs my arm and spins me around, making me laugh. He starts doing painfully bad dance moves, and I cover my eyes.

"Stop, it hurts!" I joke. He pulls me back in and puts his hand on my hips while I rest my arms around his neck.

"How has life here been?" I ask. I realized he's never actually told me what it's like living here. We've been so busy either fighting or kissing that we never actually talked about his life here.

"It's been good. Coach loves me and said that I should be able to do well in college. What about you?" he asks.

"Well, that's great! You're more talented than you think. Life in Massachusetts has been different since you left. My mom has been driving me crazy, and until I get an macceptance letter to Harvard, I don't think she'll stop," I say.

"You know I'm just a phone call away," he says.

"I know, but I want you to have fun, okay? Don't worry about me," I reassure him.

"I don't think I'll ever stop worrying about you."

CHAPTER 36

TYLER

"Ladies and gentlemen, it's time for the last dance. Grab your date and enjoy this final song. Thank you for being such a wonderful crowd," the DJ says before playing a slow song. I look at Lexi and smile.

"What?" she asks.

"I just don't know how I got so lucky," I say.

"Me either," she replies. I look at her in awe as she leans into me and sways back and forth.

"Can I kiss you?" I ask.

She looks up at me and smiles.

"You don't even have to ask." I grab the side of her cheeks and slowly bring my head to hers until our lips touch.

"Let's get out of here," I whisper in her mouth.

"Let's," she says. I smile and grab her hand while walking out.

* * *

We get back home and I take her up to my room. I shut the door and quickly kiss her again.

"What about your mom?" she asks me.

"My mom isn't here," I answer, before kissing her again.

"Tyler—" she mumbles.

"No," I cut her off, "I know what you're going to say, but we can make this work. I love you and you love me. What more do we need?"

"But—"

"Stop talking and kiss me back," I say in her mouth.

"Okay."

I smile and lift her up. I bring her face close to mine and kiss her. I lay her gently on the bed, keeping my weight off of her so I don't crush her.

"Are you sure you're ready?" I ask her. She nods her head.

"I'm ready."

* * *

I wake up with a big smile on my face. I wish last night never ended.

"Hey, beautiful," I say turning around to face her, only she's not there. I stand up and throw a shirt on. She's probably in the bathroom.

After waiting in my room for ten minutes, I figure she's downstairs with my mom. I walk downstairs to the kitchen, only to find my mom standing alone. She's in her comfy pajamas with pink slippers on, sipping her coffee.

"What's going on?" I ask her.

"You let Lexi sleep in your bed?" she questions me.

"Where is she?" I ask.

"You didn't answer my question," my mom says calmly.

"Yeah, well you didn't answer mine," I fight back. She sighs.

"Carly picked her up this morning. She's dropping Lexi off at the train station."

My eyes go wide. I grab my keys and quickly run outside.

"Tyler! Where do you think you're going? We aren't done talking about this!" my mom yells from inside.

"Yeah, well I am," I yell back, and I get in my car.

As I'm driving to the station, I keep calling Carly and Lexi, and neither are answering. I'm getting so frustrated as I keep getting their voicemail. I pull into the parking lot and run outside. Where are they? I spot Carly standing outside of the train station.

"Carly!" I shout. She turns around, and her mouth drops.

"What are you doing here?"

"I could ask the same question to you. What were you thinking?" I shout.

"Look, I'm sorry, alright? But Lexi asked me to do this. What was I supposed to say, no?" she asks me.

"Uh, yeah! I thought we were friends. I cannot believe you would do this to me," I huff.

"Tyler?" I hear a whisper coming from behind me. I turn around and face Lexi.

"What are you doing?" I ask.

"I'm going home," she says. I can tell that she's been crying by the sound of her voice.

"But you weren't supposed to leave until tomorrow," I tell her.

"I know, but I changed my mind."

"What? Why?"

"Because I can't be with you," she says, her voice cracking.

"Lexi, tell me what's wrong. I can fix it."

"No, you can't. You can't fix it. I'm sorry, but I have to go," she says.

"What do you mean? Lexi, what happened?" I ask.

"Addison was right," she mumbles.

"Addison? Who's Addison?" I ask.

"Some girl that works at the mall. She told me that she gave up everything for her boyfriend only to be dumped," Lexi says.

"You're going to base our relationship on some girl you don't even know? Are you crazy?" I yell, getting angry.

"Tyler I know you're angry, but please try to understand where I'm coming from," she says.

"You know what, screw you, Lexi. I have been trying for months for us to get back together, and you have been acting like a baby this entire time. I don't even know why I started dating you in the first place. Go back to living your pathetic life alone. I'll stay out of your life, and you stay out of mine. Good luck trying to find another guy who will put up with your crap. You're just a spoiled bitch."

I storm away.

CHAPTER 37

LEXI

I look at Carly, who has her hand over her mouth.

"Lexi—"

"No, it's fine," I say, trying my best not to cry.

"It's not fine. I'll talk to him," she says to me.

"No, please don't. Seriously, I'm okay."

She gives me a sympathetic look, then hugs me. "I never thought that I could become so close to someone that I just met."

"I know, and I hated you at first!" I attempt to joke. She backs away and looks at me.

"If you need anything, just give me a call," she says.

"I will, thank you for everything." I smile.

"I love you," she says.

"Love you, too."

She gives my arm a squeeze, then gets in her car. She waves

goodbye before driving off, leaving me to stand alone in the crowded train station.

***

I really shouldn't be by myself after what had happened. I can't believe Tyler thinks of me like that, even after everything we've been through. I've never wanted to crawl in a ball and hide more than I do now. I'm absolutely heartbroken. I have never heard him get so angry before. He hates me, he definitely made that pretty clear.

The entire train ride, I just sit and stare in front of me. My phone keeps buzzing, but I don't have the energy to look at it. It's probably from Bianca, who's picking me up from the train station. I must've dozed off, because before I know it, we are pulling up to the train station in Massachusetts. I pick up my phone and text Bianca that I'm here. I slowly walk out of the train station in Massachusetts holding my suitcase.

"Lexi!" Bianca says, giving me a hug.

"Hi," I say.

"I want to hear everything," Bianca gushes.

"Trust me, you don't," I mumble.

The first thing I do when I get home is climb into bed. I don't want to do anything except sleep and cry. I hear a gentle knock on my door and my mom opens it. I wipe away the tears on my cheek and wrap the blanket tighter around me.

"I'm about to watch a movie. Do you want to watch with me?" she asks.

"No, thanks. I'd rather stay here with my bowl of ice cream and die," I say to her.

"Do you want to talk about it?"

"No."

"I know this seems like the end of the world now, but trust me, it'll get better.

Tyler was lucky to have you, and it's his loss," my mom says to me.

"You have to say that. You're my mom."

"Alexa, we both know I'm painfully blunt. I don't have to say anything." She gives me a smile then shuts the door.

I think I'm still in shock after what Tyler said to me and haven't fully processed it yet. I didn't even recognize him. He hurt me so bad, and I don't think I will ever be able to forgive him.

* * *

After a couple weeks, I'm staring into my locker. I haven't heard from Tyler at all.

I wonder if he's even thinking about me. I haven't even heard from Carly, except for when she told me that she and Sabrina aren't friends anymore.

"Lexi," I hear through a faze. "Lexi." I snap out of it and look at the person next to me.

"I've said your name five times. Are you okay?" James asks me. Why is James talking to me? I thought he hated me.

"I guess you can say that. What's up?" I ask, shutting my locker and proceeding to walk to class.

"I just wanted to talk," he says, following me.

"Well talk," I say, still walking away.

"Lexi, will you just stop for one second?" He grabs my arm, making me come to a halt.

"What do you want, James?" I ask him.

"I wanted to apologize. I shouldn't have freaked out at you. I think deep down I always knew that you still had feelings for Tyler, but I just wanted to be with you. I'm sorry I got into things with him," he says to me.

"You're apologizing? James, I'm the one that cheated. If anyone should apologize, it should be me," I tell him.

"I just hope maybe we can be friends. I miss you."

"Yeah, I would really like that," I say, smiling.

"Cool," James says as he puffs out his chest.

"Well, I gotta get to class, but I'll talk to you later?"

"Sure thing. See you later," he says.

CHAPTER 38

TYLER

"Hey, Carly! Wait up!" I say running after her.

"Can't talk, I've got to get to practice," she says, speeding up. I grab her arm and pull her back to me.

"Okay, fine, I know you're pissed at me," I say.

"You're right, I am," she says, crossing her arms.

"She was leaving me, Carly. She was going to leave without even telling me."

"Yeah, and if I were her, I would've done the same thing," she tells me.

"What should I do?" I ask for her advice. I know I screwed up. Lexi didn't deserve that. Was I angry and hurt? Yes. But I still do love her? Very much.

"Um, you could start by apologizing," Carly suggests. She puts her cheerleading bag over her shoulder and walks away.

I take my phone out of my pocket and take a deep breath. Okay, Tyler, just say you're sorry. I click on her name, but it goes straight to voicemail. Great, she probably blocked me. I deserve it though. I can't believe I freaked out on her like that. I'm such an idiot. This whole mess started because of me. If I had simply told her that I was moving to Connecticut sooner, she wouldn't have broken up with me. In fact, she probably would have been so excited for my mom. I slowly walk back to my house with my head down and open the door.

"Tyler, we need to talk," my mom says right away.

"Not now," I grumble.

"Yes, now," she says in a stern voice.

I turn my head. I have never heard my mom sound so angry before. I sit on the counter and look at her.

"Now I don't give many rules in this house, but when I do, I expect them to be followed." I rub my hand over my face.

"I'm sorry mom, okay? Things just haven't been the best for me lately."

"And I understand that. But it's just the two of us. If we can't communicate, then how are we ever going to have a good relationship? I'm very sorry about Lexi, but you still have me, okay?" My mom says, smiling.

"Okay, I love you."

"I love you too. Now come and give me a hug," my mom says, opening her arms up to me.

CHAPTER 39

LEXI

I shut my locker just as someone comes up from behind and gives me a hug.

"Happy birthday!" Bianca says.

"Aw, thanks B."

"I can't believe you're an adult! So, what are your plans for today?" she asks me.

"Okay, get ready for this. They're very exciting. After school, I'm going to go home, order pizza, get in my pajamas, and watch a movie," I tell her.

Bianca frowns. "Oh, come on, Lexi. It's your eighteenth birthday. Do something fun!" she encourages me.

"I don't even know what fun is," I say with a shrug. It's true. I have been a workhorse from day one. Yeah, of course I had my fun with Tyler, but I'm trying to forget him.

"Okay, how about James and I go over to your house and watch the movie with you?" she suggests.

"You'd really rather do that then go out?" I ask her.

"No, but I would rather hang out with my best friend," she says with a big smile.

Wow, I never thought in a million years Bianca would call me her best friend.

"Okay, yeah, I would love for you guys to come over," I tell her.

"Great! I'll go and tell James. See you later!" She gives me another hug and skips away.

Later that night I wait for Bianca and James. I am happy they're coming, but there is a part of me that is sad. I imagined my 18th birthday to be special, with Tyler.

He would take me to a fancy restaurant and we would go and get ice cream and end the night walking on the beach. At least, that's what we talked about doing. For his eighteenth birthday we planned on going to an amusement park. I laugh at how different we are. It's crazy. The doorbell rings. I open the door and smile.

"Hey guys," I answer.

"Happy birthday," James says, giving me a hug.

"So, what movie are we watching?" Bianca asks, walking in.

"I don't know. What do you guys want to watch?" I ask.

"Isn't your favorite movie Wizard of Oz? Let's just watch that," James says, grabbing a chocolate covered strawberry that I made.

"I wouldn't make you guys watch that," I tell them.

"Lexi, it's your birthday, not ours. C'mon, let's watch it," Bianca says.

I nod my head as I sit in between James and Bianca. He grabs the remote and flips through the TV channels.

"Oh, Lexi, I forgot to tell you, Logan asked me to prom," Bianca informs me. I pop up and look at her.

"The same Logan you've had a crush on for the past ten years?" I ask her.

"It hasn't been ten years, but yes, that's the one. We should go dress shopping together!" Bianca squeals.

"Yeah, we should. Except for one problem. I'm not going." Now it's her turn to pop up.

"What do you mean you're not going?" she asks.

"Bianca, I'm known as that girl who used to date Tyler. And after that show Tyler put on with Jace in the beginning of the school year, no one is going to ask me. They're too afraid of him," I explain.

"I'll take you."

Bianca and I turn our heads at the same time and look at James.

"What are you talking about?" I ask him.

"I think I've proven in the past that I'm not afraid of Tyler. I'll be more than happy to be your prom date," James says to me.

"You'll really take me? Even after everything?" I ask him.

"Lexi, just because we broke up doesn't mean I stopped caring about you. I'd be honored to take you to prom," he says.

"Okay, yeah, I'll be your prom date," I smile

"Great! Now we can go dress shopping!" Bianca says.

***

I wake up to the sound of the door opening and closing. My head is resting on James's chest and Bianca is on the floor. I wipe my eyes and look up. We must've fell asleep watching Wizard of Oz.

My mom walks in the living room and gasps. James's eyes pop open and Bianca groans.

"What on earth is going on?" she asks.

"We were just watching a movie," I tell her.

"At one in the morning?" she asks.

"We fell asleep," I explain.

"Bianca and James, I'm sure your parents are worried. It's time for you to go home," my mom says to them.

Bianca gets up and grabs her purse. She mouths "Good luck," as James gives me a warm smile before following Bianca out. I turn the TV off and fold the blanket that was covering us.

"We aren't done discussing this," my mom says. My dad walks in the room.

"What's going on?" he asks. My mom ignores him.

"You know, I felt very bad leaving you on your birthday, but your father had a very important work party that we couldn't miss. But after what I just saw, I'm very disappointed in you," she scolds, shaking her head.

"Why? Tomorrow's Saturday," I ask, confused.

"You brought your friends over without asking for permission. That's not what a future Harvard student does."

I blink. *Are we really going to have this discussion again?*

"Well, good thing I'm not going to Harvard."

"Just go to bed Alexa. I'm too tired to have this argument with you," she demands.

I roll my eyes but do as I am told. I'm too tired to have this argument tonight.

CHAPTER 40

TYLER

I'm at another party. Yes, I know, bad things seem to always happen at parties.

I'm not exactly sure what I'm doing here, to be honest. I just think after that whole thing with Lexi, I needed to blow off some steam. I want to call her so bad, but there are two problems with that. The first one is that she blocked me. The second one is that she doesn't even want to hear from me.

"Drink, you need it," Andrew says, handing me a cup.

"Thanks," I drink the whole thing. It was her birthday today, her 18th birthday. We always thought that we would be together for our 18th birthdays. We had a plan and everything, and I couldn't even wish her a happy birthday. Honestly, a phone call from me probably would have ruined it. Why does my life have to suck?

"I'll catch you later. I think I'm going to throw up," Andrew says to me as he walks towards the bathroom.

"Woah, someone has his grumpy pants on," Carly says, walking up to me.

"I'm not grumpy. I just have a lot of things going on right now," I tell her.

"You always have a lot of things going on."

"I'm just not in the mood right now," I say to her.

"Party pooper," Carly says. I think it's pretty obvious she's a little drunk right now.

She's acting like a child.

"I think I saw that they were doing keg stands outside. You should go and check,"

I say to her.

Her eyes light up. "Okay!" she yells, and then runs away.

* * *

The next day, Ben and I are helping Carly study for her history test that she has on Tuesday. She is super hung over from the night before and can't focus as well.

"I'm tired," Carly grumbles. She tosses her books to the side and lays down on the couch.

"C'mon Carly, you just have to memorize this one section and then you're all set," I encourage her.

"Yeah, we both believe in you. You're almost done," Ben says.

"I give up," Carly says, grabbing the pillow next to her and putting it over her face.

Just then her phone rings. She groans but grabs her phone off the table and looks at it.

"Who is it?" I ask.

"No one," she says quickly. I get up and walk over to Carly.

"Is there a reason you can't tell me?" I ask, raising my eyebrows.

"I don't know what you're talking about," she says nervously. I look over her

shoulder and at her phone. Oh my god, it's Lexi. She gives me a look and answers.

"Hey, Lexi!" she says excitedly.

"Put it on speaker," I whisper. When she shakes her hand I say it again, only this

time more aggressively. She sighs, then puts it on speaker.

"What's up?" Carly asks her.

"You're not with anyone, right?" Lexi asks. I know she was asking if Carly was

with me. She looks at me and I shake my head.

"Nope," Carly lies.

"Good, wanna hear something exciting?" Lexi asks. Man it feels so good to listen to her voice. I'm glad that she doesn't sound mad anymore.

"Of course," Carly replies.

"James asked me to prom!"

I'm sorry, what? I don't think I heard her correctly. Did she say that James asked her to prom? Since when are her and James back together? Carly looks at me, then puts her hand on my thigh to stop me from exploding.

"Wow, that's exciting!" Carly says back to her.

"I know, I thought no one would ask me, but he did! It was so unexpected and romantic. It was perfect," Lexi gushes. I can feel my face turning red. I seriously want to hurt James. How dare he ask Lexi?

"That's great. Well, listen, I have to go, but we should talk on the phone more often. I miss you," Carly says to her.

"I miss you, too. I'll talk to you later, bye," Lexi says, and Carly hangs up. Carly instantly starts talking to try and calm me down.

"In a way, James is doing you a favor."

I give her a sideways look. What is she talking about?

"Look, you want Lexi to be happy, right?"

"Of course I do. Everything I ever did, I did to make her happy."

"Well going to prom will make her really happy. And now that she has a date, it will make her even more happy," Carly says. I love how she always looks on the bright side. I, however, cannot.

"I should be the one taking her, not James."

CHAPTER 41

LEXI

I'm not an idiot, I knew Tyler was listening. I heard him whisper something about putting me on speaker. I actually didn't even call to tell Carly about James. I called to ask if I left my sweatshirt there from when I visited. So yeah, I might've made up the fact that it was romantic or that it was perfect, but can you blame me? I wanted to make Tyler jealous. He deserves it.

I'm sitting at my computer writing a ten page essay on the Black Plague when my mom comes barging in my room. I look at her like a crazy person.

"Yes?" I ask.

"This is it, this could be the biggest turning point in your life. You could either be a somebody or a nobody," she says, out of breath like she just ran a mile.

"What are you talking about?" I ask, very confused as to what is happening.

"Harvard sent out their letters. Go, check your email," my mom instructs me. I do as I am told and sure enough, there's an email from Harvard.

"Oh my god," I say. My heart instantly starts beating fast. What if I didn't get in?

Will my mom disown me? Honestly, I think she would.

"Well go on, click it," my mom says, hovering over my shoulder. I think she's more nervous than I am. I take a deep breath, then click the email.

Dear Alexa Marget, On behalf of everyone at Harvard, I would like to congratulate you...

And I stopped reading. I think I went into shock. I got into Harvard? I hear my mom scream in the background. Who gets into Harvard? Oh no. What am I going to do?

* * *

"You got into Harvard?" Bianca asks the next day in school. I nod my head.

"Oh my god that's amazing! I'm so happy for you!" She gives me a hug. James comes up and asks what's going on. "You're looking at the newest Harvard student," Bianca says to him. His eyes go wide.

"What? That's incredible!" James says giving me a hug.

"Yup, so awesome," I say quietly.

"I can't wait to hear all about this Friday when I pick you up for prom. I got a tie to match your blue dress. I'll see you around, ladies." He winks at me then walks away.

"Wow, not gonna lie, that was hot," Bianca says to me. I laugh then walk away.

The day before prom, craziest time of the year. Girls are freaking out, boys are scared of the girls; it's mayhem at our school. I get tapped on my shoulder. I turn around, and it's James holding a dozen red roses.

"Beautiful flowers for the beautiful lady," James says, handing them to me. I smell them and smile.

"Aw James, that's so sweet!"

"I have another surprise for you, but you'll receive it tomorrow at prom," he says.

"You love to play games. I'll catch you later. I have to get going. USC are sending their letters tonight," I give him a hug goodbye.

"Good luck, you're gonna get in," he smiles before walking away.

I get home and go straight to my room, where I sit at my desk and stare at the wall for an hour. I watch the clock move slowly, and when it strikes five, I start to sweat.

USC sent out their letters. I go to my email, where the letter from USC waits. I don't want to click it. I only applied to two schools, here and Harvard. If I don't get in, then I'll have to go to Harvard, and I really do not want to go to Harvard.

Well, here goes nothing. I click on the link.

"I got in!" I jump up for joy as I yell. My dad comes running in.

"What's going on?"

"Dad I got in. I got into USC!" I tell him. Thank god my mom isn't here right now.

She would suck the fun right out of it.

"Oh my god, honey, that's amazing!" my dad says, giving me a hug. I have to call Carly and Bianca. They're both going to freak out.

***

The next day, Bianca comes over early to get ready. Logan and James will be picking us up in about two hours, giving us just enough time to finish primping. I think about the winter dance in Connecticut, when I went with Tyler. It was the best night of my entire life, but I try to shake those memories out of my head. Tonight, it's all about me and James, not Tyler. By the time Bianca is finished curling my hair, we have ten minutes.

"Bianca, I'm sorry," I say to her.

"For what?" she asks, confused.

"For not being a good friend. I let drama and boys get in the way of our friendship. Honestly, I couldn't have gotten through this year without you. You truly are my best friend," I say to her.

"I love you so much." She smiles and gives me a hug.

"Now let's go get in our dresses!" I say to her.

After about fifteen minutes, the doorbell rings, and Bianca and I look at each other.

"We look good," Bianca laughs. I grab my silver bracelet and Bianca helps me put it on.

"Alright, let's go." I grab Bianca's hand and we walk downstairs, trying not to fall in the heels we have on. I open the door.

"Ladies! Don't you look gorgeous," Logan says, walking inside. James gives me a hug.

"You really do look beautiful," James says, whispering into my ear and making me blush.

"Here you go," Logan says, handing Bianca a corsage.

"Aw thanks!" Bianca gushes. I look at James and raise my eyebrows.

"Well, this is awkward. I totally forgot to get one for you," James says to me.

"That's okay."

"Lexi, I'm kidding." He takes a corsage out from behind his back and hands it to me. Wow, it's so pretty. It has a dark blue ribbon wrapped around a white flower to match my dress.

"Thanks so much," I say to him.

"Let's get this show on the road!" Bianca says.

We get to the catering hall and it's already packed. James grabs my hand and we push our way through the crowd until we get in the middle of the dance floor.

"May I have this dance?" James asks me.

"Why of course," I say. I wrap my arms around his neck while he rests his hands on my hips.

"Thank you James, for everything. I wasn't a good girlfriend to you, yet you still took me to prom," I say to him.

"I wouldn't want to be here with anyone else," he replies. I smile then lay my head on his chest. About 30 minutes later we get an announcement that the band is taking a five minute break.

"I think it's time to show you your surprise. Come with me, it's just outside in the hallway." He grabs my hand and takes me there.

"You really didn't have to get me anything. This whole night has been enough," I say to him as he opens the door.

"Look," he says to me. I look in the direction he's pointing, then my eyes go wide.

There stands Carly, in a white prom dress.

"Oh my god!" I smile and give her a hug.

"I missed you so much," she says to me. Her beautiful blonde hair is curled, just like mine. She's so pretty.

"You look stunning," I say to her.

"So do you," a voice behind me says. I don't even have to turn around to know who it is. I look at James, then to Carly.

"I'll give you two some privacy," James says to me.

"Wait, you can't go back out there by yourself," I say.

"I'm not. Carly, will you be my prom date?" James asks, winking at her.

"Yes," she smiles. She links arms with James, then they walk into the prom.

CHAPTER 42

TYLER

Believe it or not, this was all James's idea. He called me one morning and said that he had a brilliant idea. One thing led to another, and here I am, standing in front of the girl of my dreams. Only, she's not looking at me. She has yet to turn around to face me.

"C'mon Lexi, look at me," I say to her. She turns around slowly and faces me.

"Why are you here?" she asks me.

"I wanted to see you," I say to her.

"You really hurt me, you know," she says.

"I know, and that was never my intention. I would never try to hurt you." When she doesn't say anything back, I ask, "Do you still love me?" I think I surprised her with that question by the face she made.

"Tyler…" she sighs.

"Just answer the question."

"You know I do, but it doesn't matter. What we had was over the moment you called me a bitch," she says.

"You know I don't think of you like that. I wouldn't have spent the last eight months trying to win you back if I thought you were a bitch. Give us another chance.

You want to be with me just as much as I want to be with you," I tell her.

"Tyler, you know it can't work. Long distance relationships never work."

"But that's where you're wrong. It won't be a long distance relationship. I heard you got into USC. We'll only be ten minutes away from each other. That was our plan from the beginning, wasn't it? What we have is worth it." I step closer and grab her hands. "I love you, Lexi, and I'm not ready to say goodbye again. Please, just give us another chance." I look straight into her eyes.

"I really don't know what to say."

"Then don't say anything, not tonight. Just," I take a deep breath, "come to prom with me."

"What?" she asks me, confused.

"We've been talking about senior prom since the day we got together. You have the dress, I have the suit. Lexi, will you go to prom with me?" I ask. After a moment of

silence, she finally whispers, "Yes."

CHAPTER 43

LEXI

The next day I go for a run, really needing the fresh air after last night. I can't believe Tyler drove all the way back for prom, and James knew all about it! Honestly, it was such a whirlwind I couldn't even tell you half of what happened.

I arrive back at my house, breathing heavily. I wipe the sweat from my forehead and open the door. I go to the fridge, grab a bottle of water, and chug it.

"Hi honey, how was last night?" my mom asks, walking down the stairs.

She's wearing her usual purple silk pajamas. Even in the mornings, she always looks so polished.

"It was great," I say.

"So listen, I have some great news. I scheduled a meeting with a woman that recently graduated from Harvard. It's on a Tuesday, so you'll have to miss school, but I think it's worth it, don't you think?"

I practically spit out the water that was in my mouth.

"You did what?" I ask her.

"I thought you'd be happy. This is an amazing opportunity. She has agreed to tell you everything you need to know. It was very hard to get in contact with her and schedule this. She is a very busy woman, you know," my mom explains.

I squint my eyes. "I can't believe you," I say, storming to my room.

I slam my door shut and pace in circles around my room. I'm fuming. Even after everything I've been through and after everything we've fought about, she's still pushing for me to go to Harvard. I have to put an end to this, now. It's finally time to tell her the truth. I hear a light knock on the door.

"What?" I snap. My mom opens the door and looks at me.

"Alexa, is everything alright? Why are you so angry? I did this for you."

"You're kidding me, right? God, I'm sick and tired of you pushing me to go to Harvard. I've had enough, mother." I made sure to emphasize on the word 'mother' to make sure to really get my point across on how angry I am.

"This isn't about me. This is about you getting the best possible education and future you can get. Why can't you understand that?" she asks me.

"Oh, please, you never cared about me. You care about the idea of me. You care more about what makes you look good. Just admit it, mom." I cross my arms.

"How can you say that?" my mom gasps. "Everything I have ever done was for you. When you're a mom, you'll finally understand.

But until then, you don't have the right to speak to me like this."

"Mom, I got into USC!" I spit out. I quickly cover my mouth with my hands. This is not how I wanted to tell her. I am such an idiot. Why do I always say things without thinking first?

"Well, of course you did. If you can get into Harvard, then you can get into USC," my mom says like it's obvious

"No, mom, I don't think you fully understand. I'm going to USC," I say.

"Ha! And you think you have a choice? How cute," my mom says.

"Well, it is my life, and I think I do have a say in what I do with my future," I point out.

"Alexa, all I have ever wanted for you is to succeed. By going to USC, you're throwing away all of your hopes and dreams. Please just trust me on this," she begs.

"No, mom, I'm throwing away your hopes and dreams. I don't have to go to some ivy league school to be successful. I don't even want to go to law school. Please, mom, just listen to me for once. I really, really want to go to USC."

"But Alexa, I'm your mother and I know what is best for you," she says.

"I know what's best for me, too. I'm not a child anymore. Stop being my manager for once in your life and just start being my mom."

She looks at me. "Is that really what you think of me?" she asks quietly. I realize I've hit a soft spot with her. I'm not sure why, but I could tell that calling her my manager actually hurt her.

"Sometimes," I admit.

"Oh my god, I turned into my mother," she says, looking away.

"What are you talking about?" I ask her.

"My mother always wanted me to do things her way, and I went along with it because, well, I never had the courage to tell her otherwise. Is that really how I've made you feel?"

"I mean, yeah," I say.

"Oh dear. I've failed as a mother," she frowns. My eyes go wide.

"What? No, mom, you didn't fail me. I am who I am today because of you," I say sincerely.

"Alexa, I want you to be completely honest with me. Will this really, truly, make you happy?"

"More than anything."

"Okay, I still think that Harvard is the best option, but you're an adult now. If you want to go to USC, then go to USC. I won't stop you," she tells me. A smile grows on my face.

"Really?" I ask, still in shock.

"Really. I love you, Alexa, and I know I don't say it often, but I am so proud of you and the woman you're becoming." She gives me a hug.

"I love you, too," I say.

She smiles at me one more time and squeezes my arm. "Well, I better go and shower. I have that lunch meeting with my boss in an hour and a half," she says.

She starts walking out of my room but I stop her. "Mom," I say. She turns around to face me. "Can I ask you for your advice?" She nods her head and walks back into my room.

"Tyler came to my prom last night, and he told me he still loved me. He wants to start a life with me in California. I just don't know what to do. He hurt me, mom," I tell her.

"Well, honey, you know how I feel about Tyler. That boy is trouble," she says. I nod my head and look down.

"But it's not about what I think," I hear her say. I look up. "Alexa do you still love him?"

"I don't know," I say.

She sits next to me and grabs my hand. "I think you do know. My best advice I can give you as a mother is to follow your heart. I really do have to get ready now, but if you want something, go and get it before it's too late."

She squeezes my hand before standing up and walking out of the room. I sit on my bed and rub my hand over my face. My mom's right. All I have to do is follow my heart. That should be easy, right? My mind shifts back to the fact that my mom is actually on my side for once. I can't believe I did it. I finally convinced her to give me a chance. I can't even describe how I feel. My whole life I've been fighting with my mom, and now I feel like we're finally on the same page. It's honestly a miracle, and I never thought this day would come. There's a knock on the front door, and since my mom is in the shower and I think my dad is still sleeping, I'm forced to walk downstairs and open the door.

I swing open the large glass door and on my porch stands the most handsome man alive, Tyler. He looks up at me and gives me a small smile. His hands are in his pockets and he has his hat on backwards, like always. Every time I see him I still get butterflies in my stomach. As I stare at the boy in front of me, I know exactly what I want.

"Hi, Lexi," he says awkwardly.

"Tyler, what are you doing here?" I ask him. I step outside and close the door behind me.

"I just came to say goodbye. I have to go back to Connecticut, and I don't know when I'll be back. I'll probably stay down there until I leave for California in the fall, so I don't know when I'll see you again. Carly's waiting for me in the car, so I probably should go," he says.

"Oh," I mumble. He smiles at me, then turns around and walks down the stairs.

"Tyler," I call out. He turns around and waits for me to continue. I walk down the stairs and face him. "Thank you for last night. It truly was magical," I say.

"Well, you always said you wanted to feel like a princess at your prom." Aw, he remembered our conversation we had. I couldn't go to junior prom because I was sick, so Tyler and I just stayed on the couch and watched movies while he rubbed my back.

He's always been so thoughtful and generous.

"I miss you," I blurt out. Well, this isn't how I wanted this talk to go.

"You miss me?" he asks, biting his lip.

"Here's the thing. My mom told me to follow my heart, and well, not to be overthe- top romantic or anything, but clearly my heart wants to be with you. Please say something before I have completely embarrassed myself," I say, holding my breath.

"Wait, I thought your mom hated me," he says.

"Well, she does. But she also loves me. Tyler, I'm going to California. I'm not going to Harvard. I'm coming with you," I tell him. He stumbles backwards.

"You… you're going to USC?" he stutters.

I nod my head. "Tyler, I choose you. I love you, and I honestly can't imagine my life without you. It has sucked without you here," I tell him truthfully.

"Awwww," I hear coming from behind Tyler. We both turn our heads, and there stands Carly, staring at us. She covers her mouth. "I'm so sorry, please continue," Carly says.

Tyler turns back to face me. He steps closer and grabs my hands. "So, would it be appropriate to kiss you now?" He asks me, and I smile.

"You can kiss me as many times as you want."

He cups my chin and slowly lifts my head up to his. We share a passionate, long, overdue kiss. I back my head away and look at him.

"This doesn't mean I forgive you," I say to him.

He laughs. "It's okay, I've got a long time to earn your forgiveness," and he pulls me into another kiss.

Made in the USA
Middletown, DE
09 August 2020